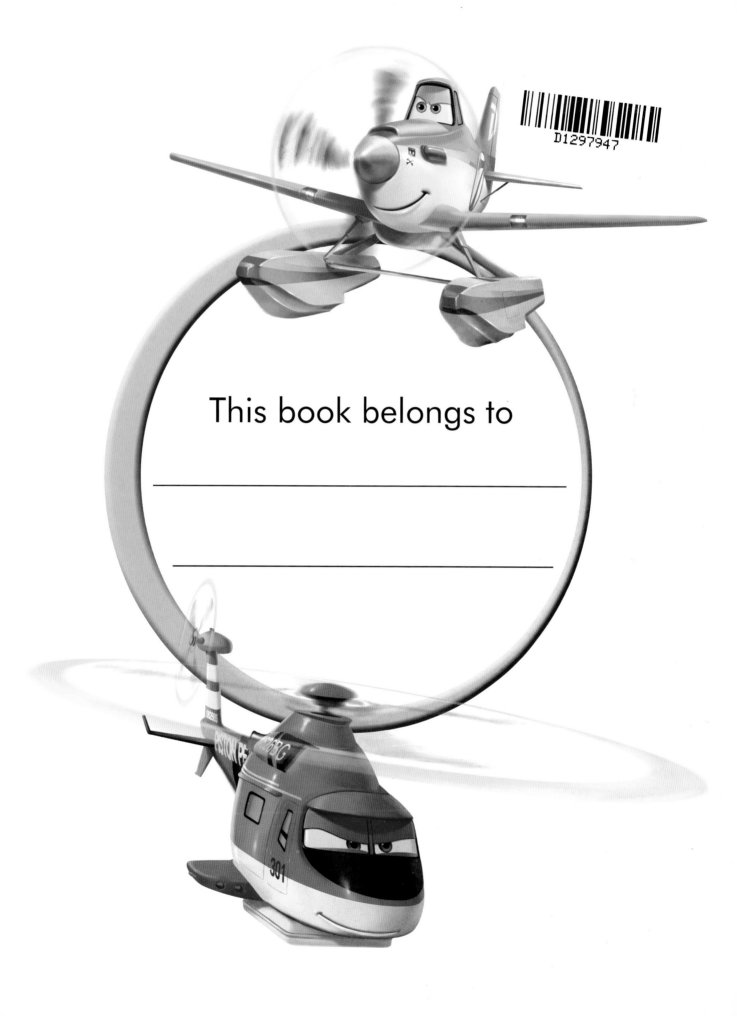

This book belongs to

_____

_____

Disney

Boys' Big Book of Fun
Time for Adventure

Pages 6–17, 34–49, 66–81, 98–101 | PLANES, THE MOVIE STORY
Based on the graphic novel by Alessandro Sisti. Layout by Roberto
Di Salvo, Grafimated, Lucio Leoni. Pencils by Lucio Leoni, Gianfranco
Florio, Paco Desiato. Paints by Massimo Rocca, Paco Desiato. Artist
Coordination by Tomatofarm.
Page 27 | HIGH FASHION
Script by Alessandro Sisti, pencils & inks by Valentino Forlini, color by
Lucio de Giuseppe.
Page 89 | MULTI-ARTIST
Script by Alessandro Sisti, pencils & inks by Valentino Forlini, color by
Lucio de Giuseppe.
Pages 102–105 | MATER'S SPECIALTY!
Script by Alessandro Sisti, pencils by Valentino Forlini, inks by Michela
Frare, color by Kawaii Creative Studio.
Pages 140–143 | TOY GAMES
Script by Alessandro Ferrari, pencils by Luca Usai, inks by Michela
Frare, color by Angela Capolupo.
Page 144 | BONNIE'S SPA
Script by Tea Orsi, pencils by Luca Usai, inks by Michela Frare, color by
Angela Capolupo.
Pages 161–165 | NICE TO GLOW YA!
Based on the series created by Dan Povenmire & Jeff "Swampy"
Marsh. Written by Scott Peterson, pencils & inks by Anthony
Vukojevich, colors by Wes Dzioba, letters by Michael Stewart.
Pages 166–169 | MULTICOLOR DISASTER
Script by Gabriele Panini, pencils by Valentino Forlini, inks by Michela
Frare, color by Kawaii Creative Studio.

This edition published by Parragon Books Ltd in 2015 and distributed by

Parragon Inc.
440 Park Avenue South, 13th Floor
New York, NY 10016
www.parragon.com

ISBN 978-1-4748-1171-2

Printed in China

Disney

Boys' Big Book of Fun
Time for Adventure

Parragon

Bath • New York • Cologne • Melbourne • Delhi
Hong Kong • Shenzhen • Singapore • Amsterdam

Planes: The Movie Story

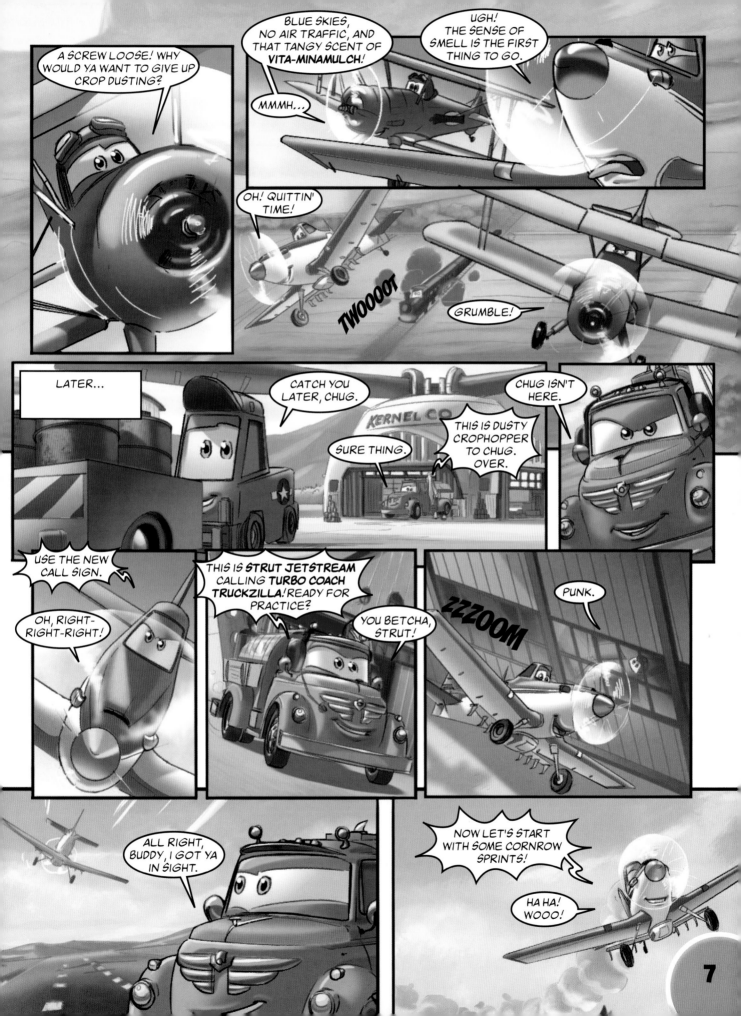

NOW LET'S TRY SOME TREE LINE MOGULS.

UH HUH!

ADJUST YOUR ANGLE OF BANK WITH YOUR **ALIEN-IRONS**...

UH?

YOU MEAN **AILERONS?**

OH... YEAH. RIGHT.

AW, GREAT.

SPUTT SPUTT

YOU'VE WORN OUT YOUR MAIN BEARING OIL SEAL.

REALLY?

THAT KIND OF DAMAGE COMES FROM **HIGH** SPEEDS!

BUT YOU'RE A CROP DUSTER AND ALL YOU DO IS DUST CROPS AT **VERY LOW SPEEDS.**

YEP. LOW AND SLOW.

UNLESS YOU'VE BEEN... **RACING AGAIN!**

ME? **NOOO!**

THAT'S **SPEED!** WHERE A SATURN ROCKET COULDN'T CATCH YA, DUSTER!

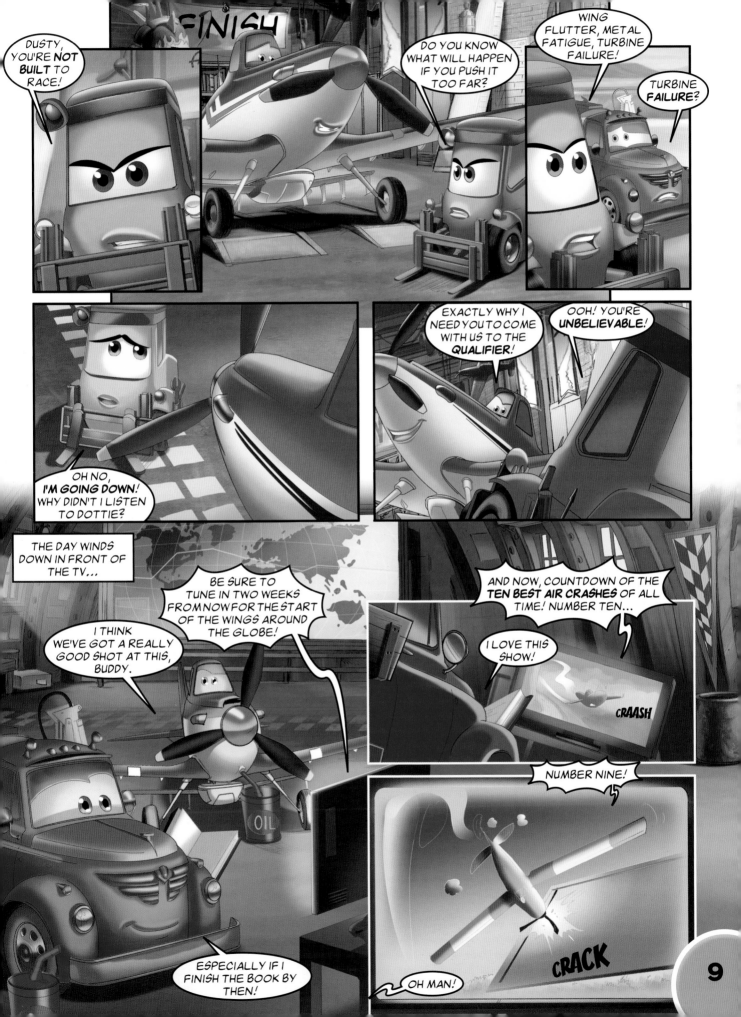

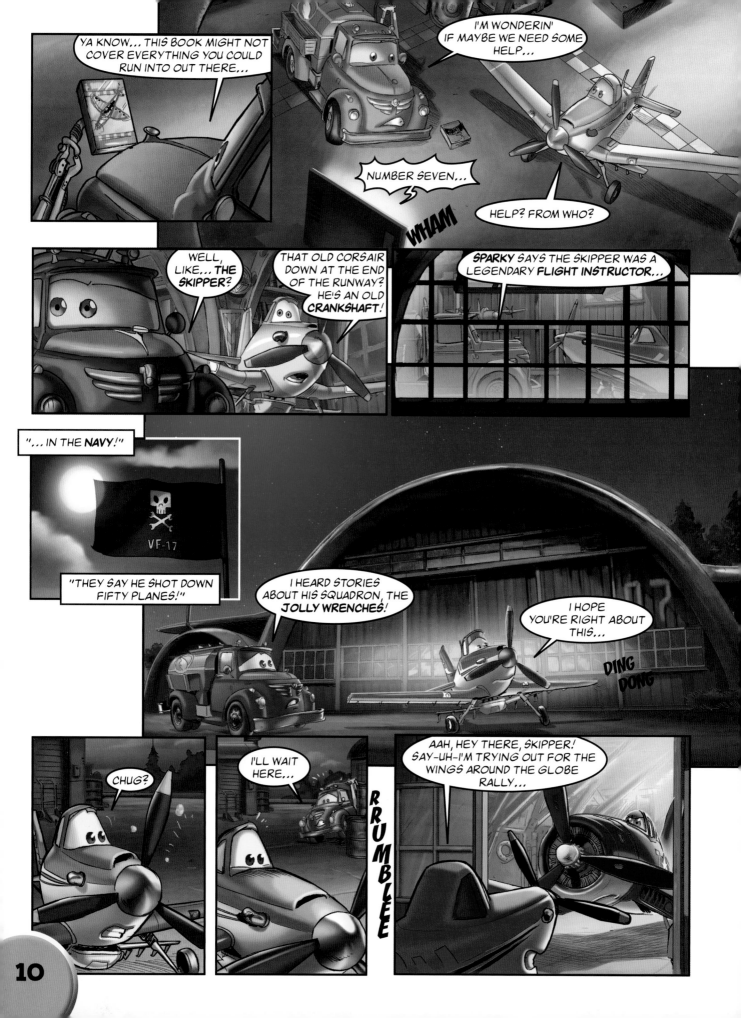

10

OH MAN! A SEA FURY!

CHECK IT OUT!

LADIES AND GENTLEPLANES...

...GIVE A WARM WELCOME TO OUR SPECIAL GUEST!

BRROAAM

RIP-SLING-A! GET MY GOOD SIDE, FELLAS!

FLASH FLASH FLASH FLASH FLASH

WITH ALL THAT SELF-PROMOTION AT LEAST HE'S MODEST...

DOTTIE! THAT'S RIPSLINGER!

HE'S CAPTAIN OF TEAM RPX! THEY CALL HIM... ...THE GREEN TORNADO!

AND THOSE OTHER TWO, NED AND ZED...

...THE TWIN TURBOS! THEY'RE WORLD CLASS RACERS!

GROAN...

THIS IS THE LAST OF FOUR TIME TRIALS BEING HELD WORLDWIDE.

THE TOP FIVE FINISHERS WILL QUALIFY FOR THE WINGS AROUND THE GLOBE RALLY!

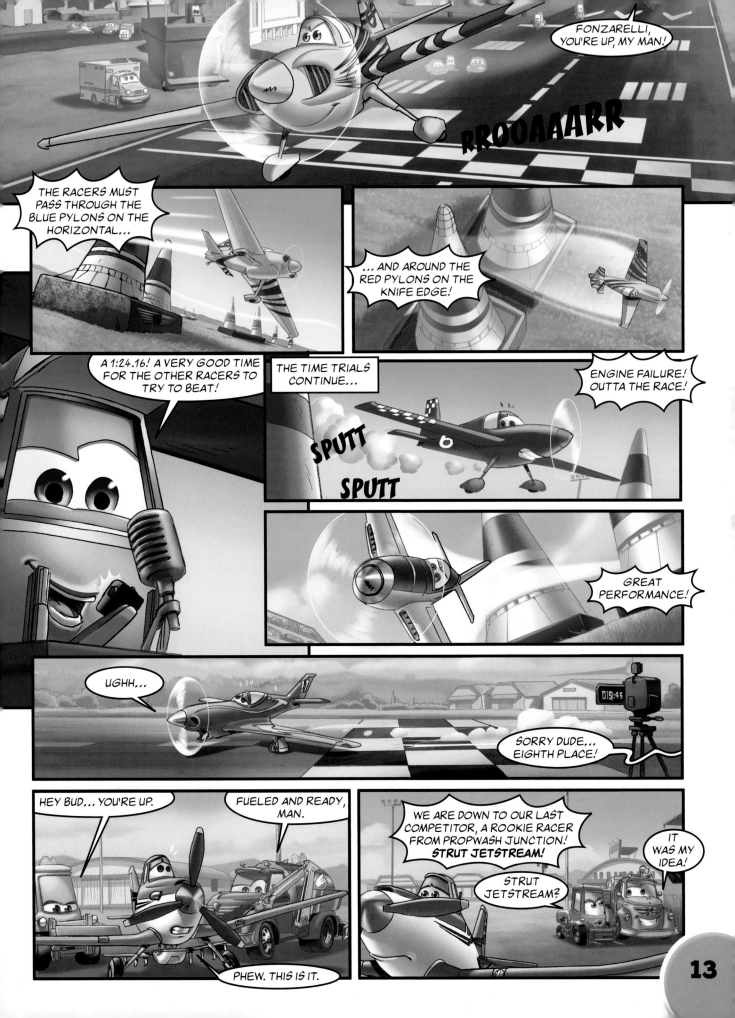

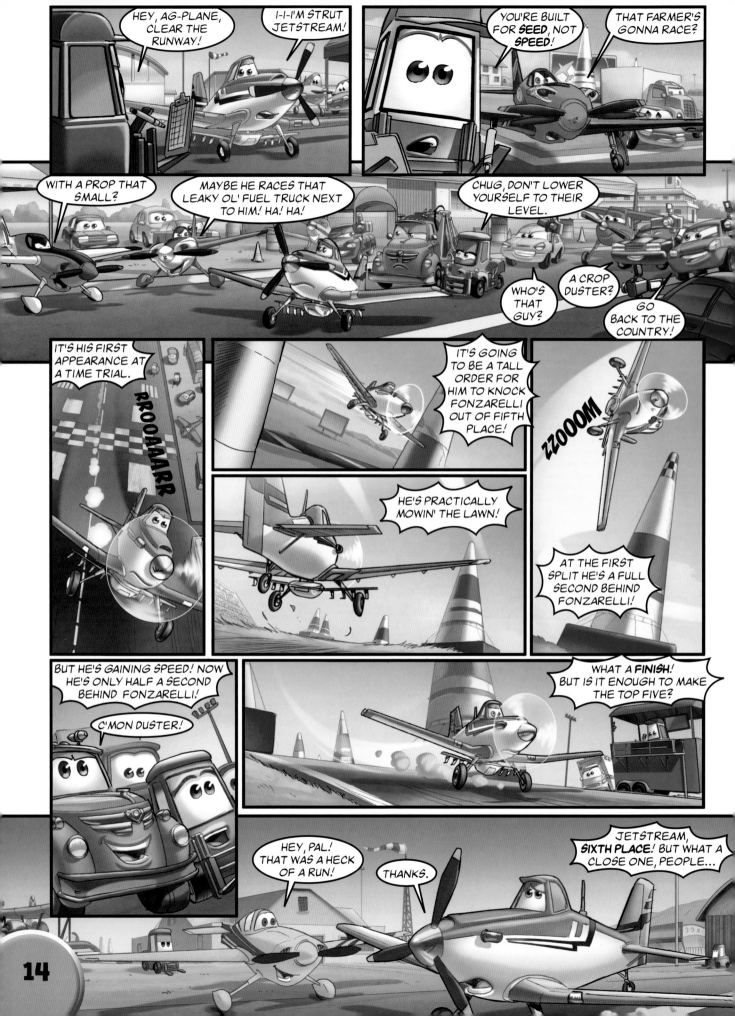

"...THAT WRAPS UP THE TRY OUTS FOR THE WINGS AROUND THE GLOBE RALLY."

E NEXT DAY...

THERE YOU GO! TOPPED OFF AND ALL SET, MAYDAY!

PLEASE TELL ME THIS IS PROPWASH JUNCTION?

SURE IS!

COUGH! I'M LOOKING FOR STRUT JETSTREAM!

ME! THAT'S ME!

BUT YOU'RE MISPRONOUNCING IT SLIGHTLY. IT'S ACTUALLY PRONOUNCED... DUSTY CROPHOPPER!

WHATEVER, DUSTY CROPHOPPER... SNIFF! WHAT IS THAT SMELL?

IT'S VITA-MINAMULCH...

THE FINEST SMELLING COMPOST THIS SIDE OF THE MISSISSIPPI!

I GOT SOME MINAMULCH, YEAH!

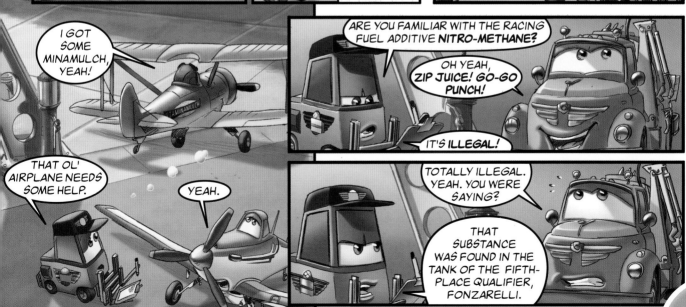

ARE YOU FAMILIAR WITH THE RACING FUEL ADDITIVE NITRO-METHANE?

OH YEAH, ZIP JUICE! GO-GO PUNCH!

IT'S ILLEGAL!

THAT OL' AIRPLANE NEEDS SOME HELP.

YEAH.

TOTALLY ILLEGAL. YEAH. YOU WERE SAYING?

THAT SUBSTANCE WAS FOUND IN THE TANK OF THE FIFTH-PLACE QUALIFIER, FONZARELLI.

MARTIAL ARTS!

SHU TODOROK[...]

1 KARATE CHOP

THIS SEQUENCE OF BOARDS APPEARS THREE TIMES IN THE GRID BELOW: ONCE HORIZONTALLY, ONCE VERTICALLY, AND ONCE DIAGONALLY. FIND THEM AND CIRCLE EACH WITH A PENCIL TO BREAK THEM WITH THREE PERFECT KARATE CHOPS.

KARATE HEADBAND[...]

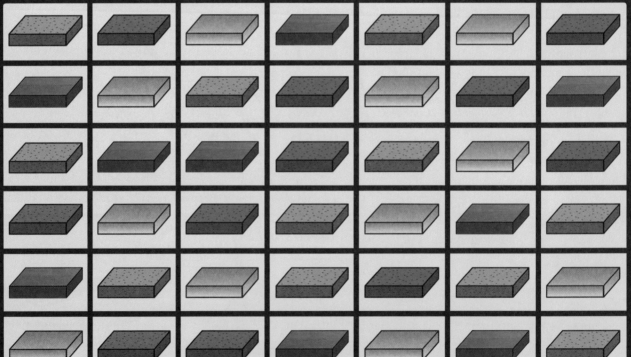

2 SUMO TUG-OF-WAR

A GAME FOR TWO PLAYERS. YOU'LL NEED ONE COIN. THE OBJECT OF THE GAME IS TO WIN THIS TUG-OF-WAR. TAKE TURNS FLIPPING THE COIN, FOR A TOTAL OF FIVE TURNS EACH. MARK ONE POINT ON YOUR SCOREBOARDS FOR EACH "HEADS" AND TWO POINTS FOR EACH "TAILS." ADD UP YOUR POINTS AFTER COMPLETING FIVE TURNS. THE PLAYER WITH THE MOST TOTAL POINTS WINS.

KIMURA KAIZO

KINGPIN NOBUNAGA

PINION TANAKA

KINGPIN SCOREBOARD

PINION SCOREBOARD

 + + + ... + ... =   ... + ... + ... + ... + ... =

3 zen maze

IMPROVE YOUR CONCENTRATION. FIND YOUR WAY OUT OF THE MAZE CREATED BY THE ZEN MASTER.

START

zen master

FINISH

Answer on page 171

I Love Japan

1

JAPANESE TUNING

LOOK AT THE TWO PICTURES BELOW. THERE ARE SEVEN DIFFERENCES BETWEEN THEM. FIND THEM ALL AND CIRCLE THEM WITH A PENCIL!

2

SUSHI MASTER

FIND THE RIGHT INGREDIENTS FOR EACH OF THE THREE SUSHI DISHES AMONG THE SEVEN SHOWN HERE.

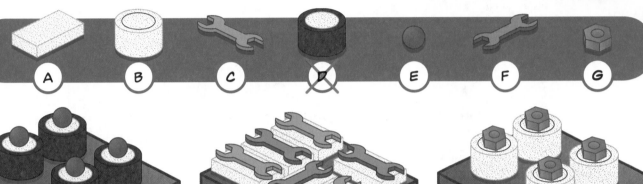

A   B   C   ~~D~~   E   F   G

1 (D) (...)

2 (...) (...) (...)

3 (...) (...)

3

TOKYO'S BROKEN LIGHTS

THE ELECTRONIC BILLBOARDS ARE MISSING FIVE DETAILS. FIND THEM IN THE PICTURES UNDERNEATH.

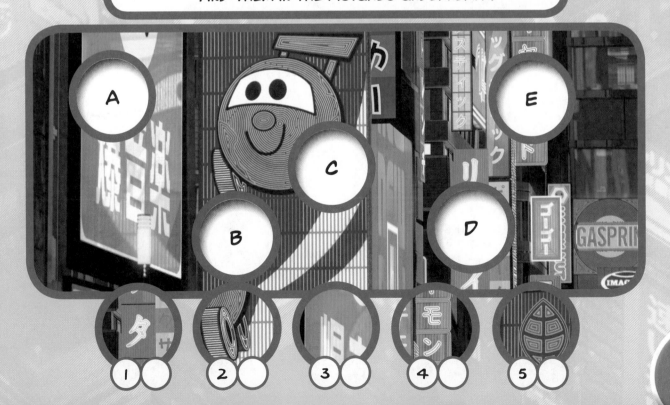

Answers on page 171

DINOS AT PLAY

The dinosaurs are playing a prehistoric game. Match each of these dinosaurs to their shadows before they become extinct! Which dinosaur does not have a shadow?

Dinosaur: ___ does not have a shadow.

Practice your dinosaur roa... ROOOOAR!

PREHISTORIC HUNT!

THE CHASE IS ON!

What type of dinosaur is Rex?

MISSION ACCOMPLISHED!
COLOR WHEN FINISHED.

Answers on page 171

22

MONSTER MAZE

Chunk and Sparks are having fun racing around Sunnyside Daycare. See if you can help them get through the maze to Lotso.

MISSION ACCOMPLISHED!

COLOR WHEN FINISHED.

START

FINISH

Answer on page 171

23

SUNNYSIDE QUIZ

The toys have been thinking up some questions about their time at Sunnyside. Test yourself with this ultimate quiz.

1

Which of these isn't a member of Lotso's crew?
A) Mr. Potato Head
B) Big Baby
C) Stretch

2

What's the name of the playroom for the younger children?
A) Butterfly Room
B) Moth Room
C) Caterpillar Room

3

What's Lotso's full name?
A) Lots-o'-Cuddles Bear
B) Lots-o'-Hug Bear
C) Lots-o'-Huggin' Bear

Where does Ken live at Sunnyside?
Barbie's Dreamhouse
B) A Dreamhouse
C) The Sandbox

5 What's the name of the robot at Sunnyside Daycare?
A) Sparks
B) Stretch
C) Twitch

6 Who has the muscles on Lotso's team?
A) Chunk
B) Big Baby
C) Ken

CHECK THE BOX WHEN YOU FIND EACH TOY IN THE BIG PICTURE.

The Aliens

Buzz & Jessie

Woody & Bullseye

Mr. & Mrs. Potato Head

Barbie & Ken

WHICH TOY DOESN'T HAVE A PICTURE ABOVE?

_ _ _ _ _ _ _ _ _ _

MISSION ACCOMPLISHED!
COLOR WHEN FINISHED.

Answers on page 171

25

COWBOY COLORING

Woody wants to play. Draw your own cowboy scene behind Woody and color his picture so he can get started.

LET'S PLAY!

MISSION ACCOMPLISHED!

COLOR WHEN FINISHED.

LET'S COLOR!

MISSION ACCOMPLISHED!

COLOR WHEN FINISHED.

HIGH FASHION

THE END

TRICKS & PRANKS!

1

ROAD SIGN RUIN

BOOST HAS STAINED A PART OF EACH ROAD SIGN. HELP MATER AND LIGHTNING TO MATCH THE SHAPES TO THE WORDS BELOW TO DISCOVER WHAT THE SIGNS SAY.

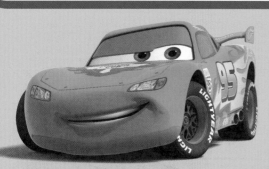

1. CASA DELLA

2. FLO'S V8

3. CONE MOTEL

4. HOUSE OF THE ART

5. DEPARTMENT

6. DRIVE-IN

 FIRE — A ...

 THEATER — B ...

BODY — C ...

TIRES — D ...

COZY — E ...

CAFÉ — F ...

28

2 SAME OLD JOKE

MATER AND LIGHTNING HAVE GONE TRACTOR TIPPING AGAIN. PUT THE FOLLOWING PICTURES IN ORDER TO SEE HOW THIS TRACTOR TIPS, BEGINNING WITH 'A' AND FINISHING WITH 'F', NUMBERING EACH LETTER IN THE RIGHT ORDER. THE FIRST ONE HAS BEEN DONE FOR YOU.

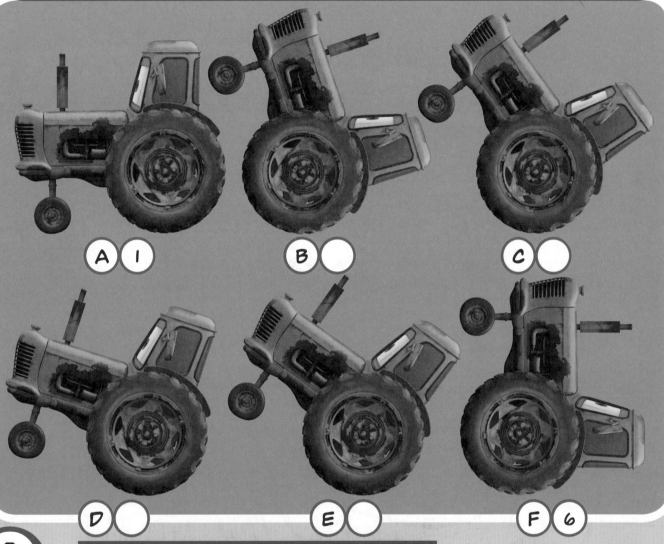

A 1   B   C

D   E   F 6

3 WHAT GOES AROUND COMES AROUND!

THIS TIME THE JOKE'S ON MATER AND LIGHTNING. SOMEONE'S MIXED THE CAPS FOR THE VALVES OF THEIR INNER TUBES WITH THE ONES BELOW. BASED ON THE ORIGINALS SHOWN HERE, FIND FOUR OF EACH KIND.

MATER   LIGHTNING

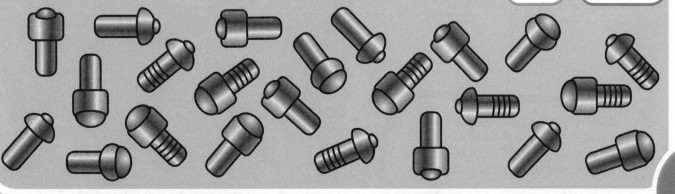

Answers on page 171

ADD SOME COLORS TO THIS
SCENE! TAKE INSPIRATION
FROM THIS PICTURE, OR LET YOUR
IMAGINATION RUN WILD!

GREM'S COLORS

I'M A LEMON, BUT I LIKE ORANGE.

HERE ARE THE COLORS YOU'LL NEED:

 SAND

 LIGHT ORANGE

 ORANGE

 GREEN

 BROWN

 DARK GRAY

LIGHT GRAY

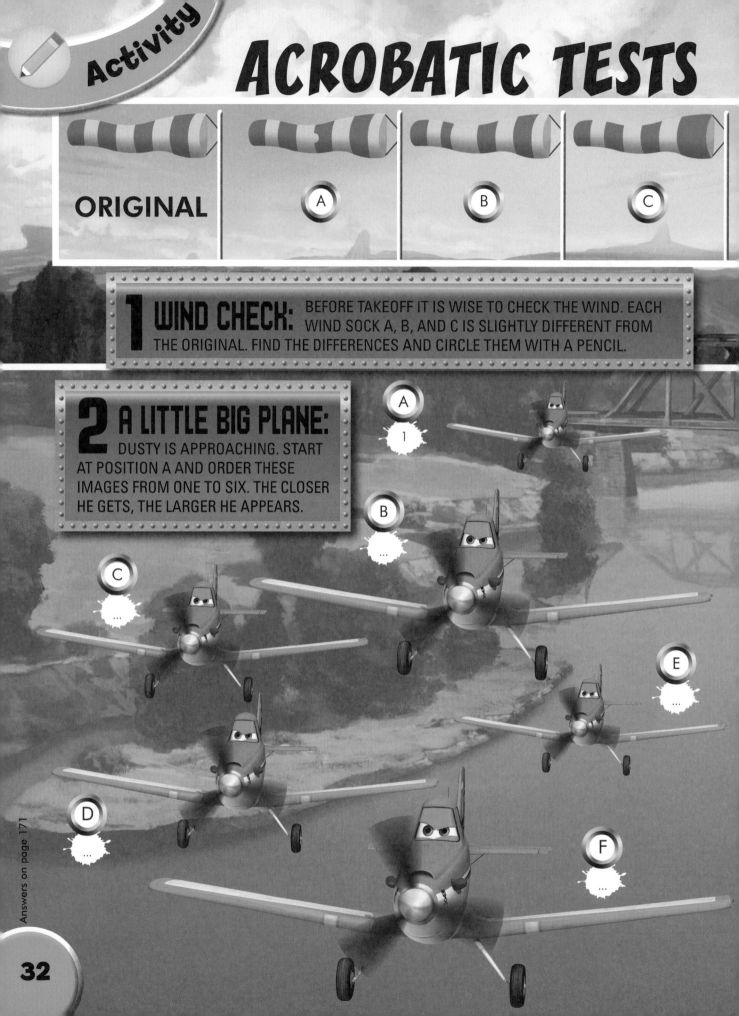

Activity

ACROBATIC TESTS

ORIGINAL | A | B | C

1 WIND CHECK:
BEFORE TAKEOFF IT IS WISE TO CHECK THE WIND. EACH WIND SOCK A, B, AND C IS SLIGHTLY DIFFERENT FROM THE ORIGINAL. FIND THE DIFFERENCES AND CIRCLE THEM WITH A PENCIL.

2 A LITTLE BIG PLANE:
DUSTY IS APPROACHING. START AT POSITION A AND ORDER THESE IMAGES FROM ONE TO SIX. THE CLOSER HE GETS, THE LARGER HE APPEARS.

A
1

B
...

C
...

E
...

D
...

F
...

3 AIR CONTEST: STUNT TIME! FOLLOW DUSTY'S AND TWO OF THE WATG RACERS' PATHS TO THE FINISH LINE AND ADD UP THEIR POINTS AS YOU GO. THEN RANK THEM BASED ON THEIR SCORES.

Ⓐ DUSTY

Ⓑ EL CHUPACABRA

Ⓒ RIPSLINGER

Answers on page 171

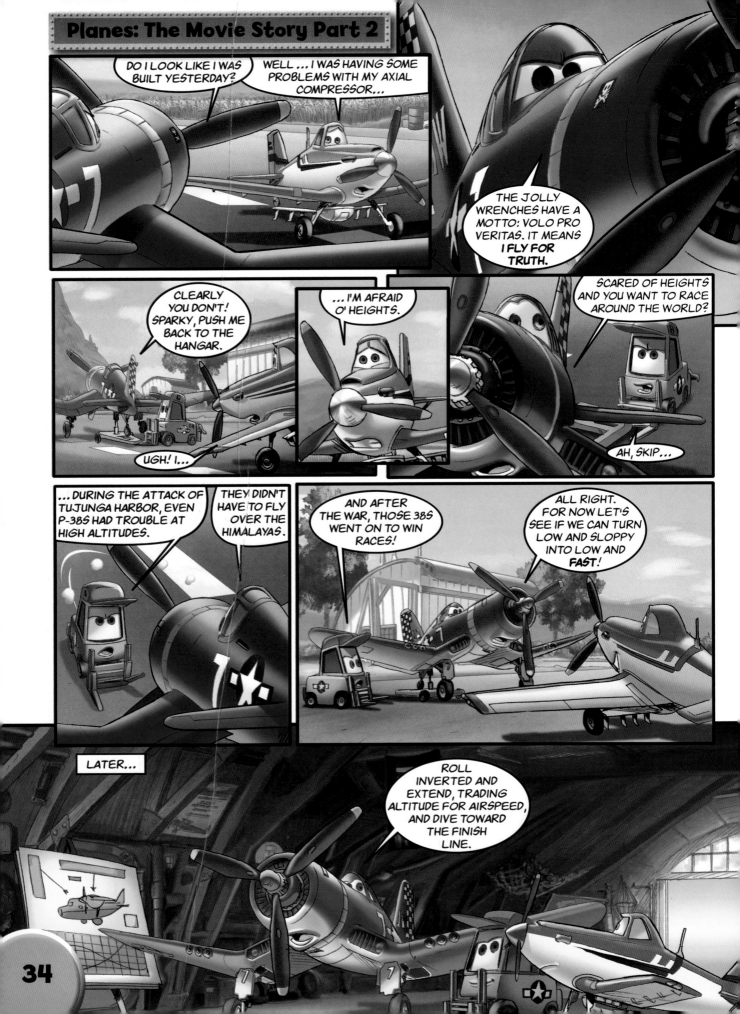

DO I LOOK LIKE I WAS BUILT YESTERDAY?

WELL ... I WAS HAVING SOME PROBLEMS WITH MY AXIAL COMPRESSOR...

THE JOLLY WRENCHES HAVE A MOTTO: VOLO PRO VERITAS. IT MEANS I FLY FOR TRUTH.

CLEARLY YOU DON'T! SPARKY, PUSH ME BACK TO THE HANGAR.

UGH! I...

... I'M AFRAID O' HEIGHTS.

SCARED OF HEIGHTS AND YOU WANT TO RACE AROUND THE WORLD?

AH, SKIP...

... DURING THE ATTACK OF TUJUNGA HARBOR, EVEN P-38S HAD TROUBLE AT HIGH ALTITUDES.

THEY DIDN'T HAVE TO FLY OVER THE HIMALAYAS.

AND AFTER THE WAR, THOSE 38S WENT ON TO WIN RACES!

ALL RIGHT. FOR NOW LET'S SEE IF WE CAN TURN LOW AND SLOPPY INTO LOW AND FAST!

LATER...

ROLL INVERTED AND EXTEND, TRADING ALTITUDE FOR AIRSPEED, AND DIVE TOWARD THE FINISH LINE.

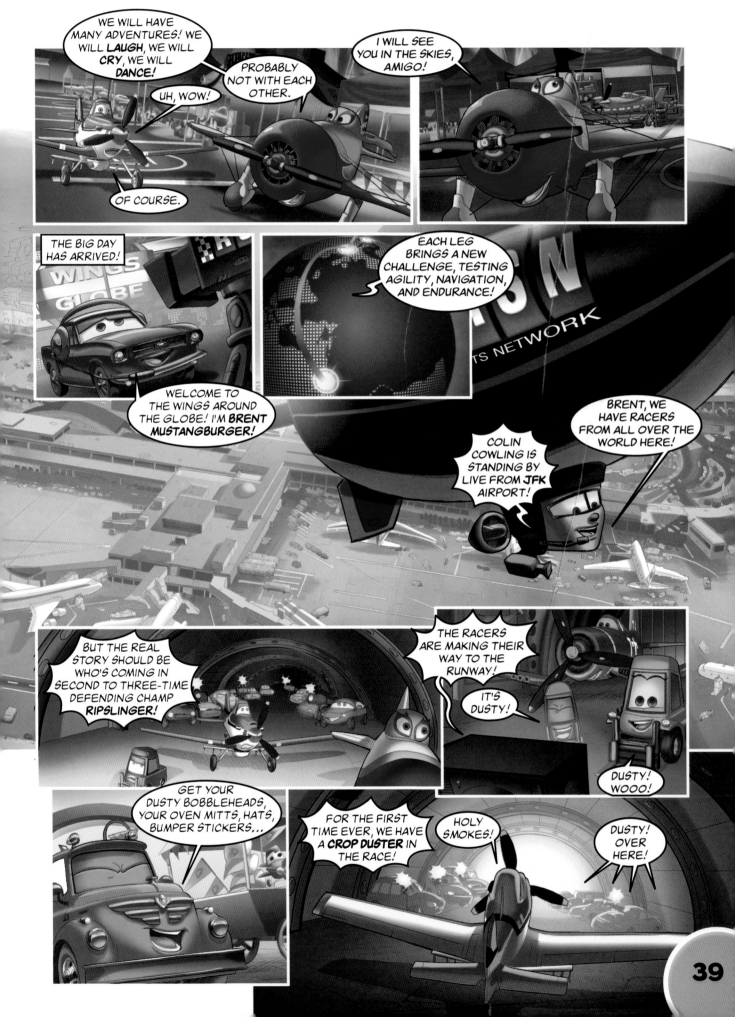

A CROP DUSTER?

WELL, HE'S GONNA DIE.

RIPSLINGER!

RIPSLINGER!

YEAH! CAUGHT IN THE RIP-TIDE!

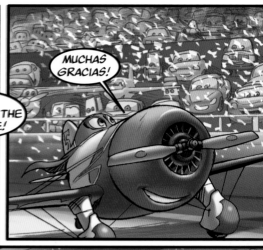

MUCHAS GRACIAS!

LOOK AT THIS CROWD...

STAY FOCUSED, AMIGO. DON'T LET ANYTHING DISTRACT YOU...

...AY! WHO IS THAT VISION?

OH, THAT'S ROCHELLE, THE CANADIAN RALLY CHAMP.

SHE'S LIKE AN ANGEL SENT FROM HEAVEN...

RACERS, START YOUR ENGINES!

OVER 19,000 MILES, THE WORLD'S HIGHEST MOUNTAINS, AND THE DEEPEST OCEANS ALL STAND BEFORE THEM!

VROOOM

GO!

WHOA! SWIRLIES!

RROOOAARR

OUR FIRST STAGE IS A WHOPPER...

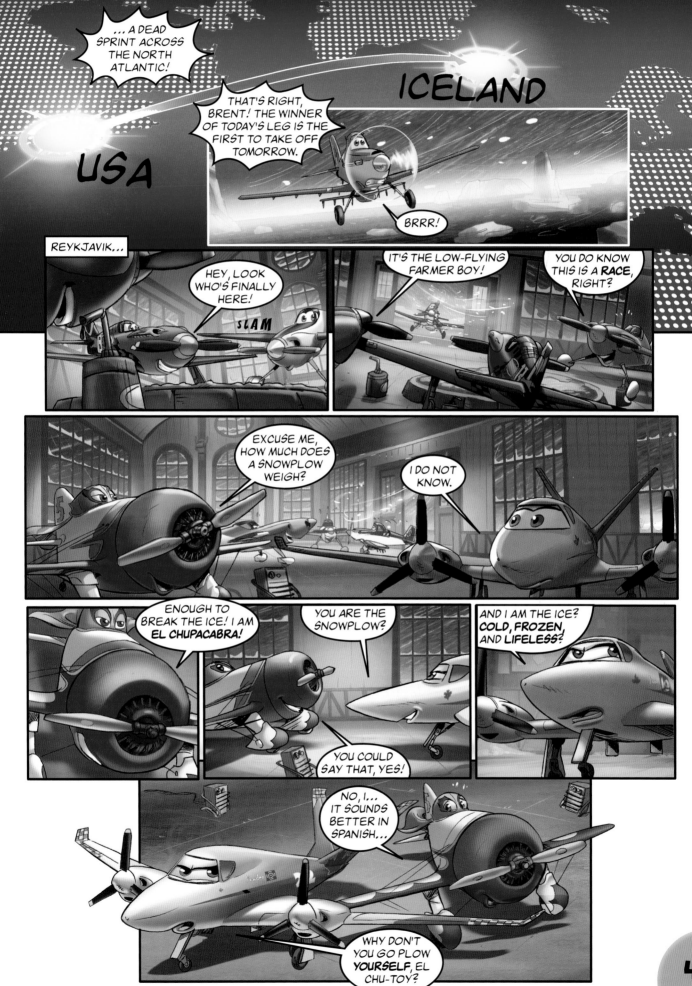

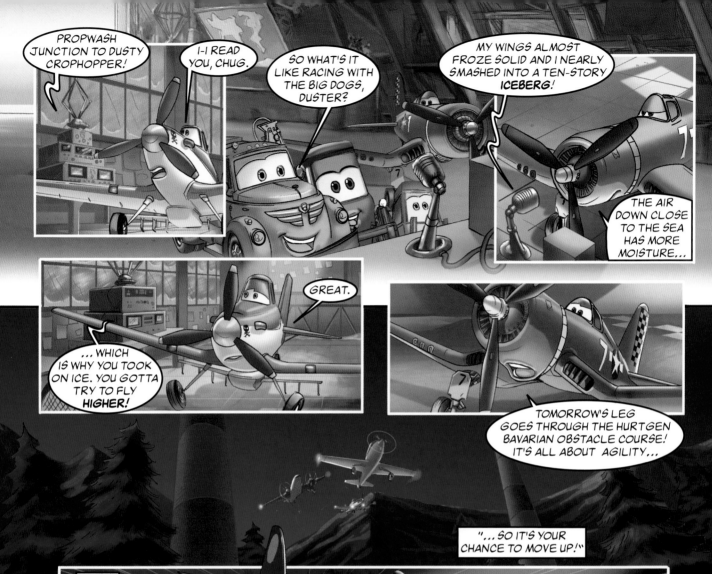

PROPWASH JUNCTION TO DUSTY CROPHOPPER!

I-I READ YOU, CHUG.

SO WHAT'S IT LIKE RACING WITH THE BIG DOGS, DUSTER?

MY WINGS ALMOST FROZE SOLID AND I NEARLY SMASHED INTO A TEN-STORY *ICEBERG!*

THE AIR DOWN CLOSE TO THE SEA HAS MORE MOISTURE,...

...WHICH IS WHY YOU TOOK ON ICE. YOU GOTTA TRY TO FLY **HIGHER!**

GREAT.

TOMORROW'S LEG GOES THROUGH THE HURTGEN BAVARIAN OBSTACLE COURSE! IT'S ALL ABOUT AGILITY...

"...SO IT'S YOUR CHANCE TO MOVE UP!"

BUT...

SPLOSH

AAGH!

BANG

MAYDAY! MAYDAY! I CAN'T *SEE!*

WE'RE RECEIVING BREAKING NEWS OF AN INCIDENT INVOLVING ONE OF THE RACERS!

YES, BRENT! BULLDOG, THE FLYER FROM THE UK, IS IN TREMENDOUS DANGER!

IT LOOKS LIKE HE'S FLYING BLIND!

I NEED ASSISTANCE! IS ANYONE THERE?

WAIT! IT'S CROPHOPPER PULLING UP BESIDE HIM!

WHAT'S HE DOING?

BULLDOG! APPLY YOUR LEFT AILERON!

OKAY

STOP ROLL. NOW QUICK, PULL UP...

WHOA! BIG CASTLE!

PULL UP, HARD ROLL RIGHT!

VROOOAM

ARE YOU STILL THERE?

I'M RIGHT HERE. I'LL FLY RIGHT ALONGSIDE YOU.

AT THE MUNICH AIRPORT...

ACHTUNG! CLEAR THE RUNWAY!

MUNICH

ADD POWER... FLAPS DOWN... LANDING GEAR DOWN!

DOWN AND LOCKED!

CHIRP

CHIRP

THANKS FOR YOUR HELP, I...

SPLAASH

...YOU? WHAT DID I TELL YOU, BOY? EVERY PLANE FOR HIMSELF.

WHERE I COME FROM, IF YOU SEE SOMEONE FALLING FROM THE SKY...

BUT THIS IS A COMPETITION! NOW YOU'RE DEAD LAST... AND I OWE YOU MY LIFE!

BULLDOG!

CAN WE GET A FEW WORDS?

I GOTTA SAY, CROP DUSTER, YOU ARE A NICE GUY.

HEY, THANKS, RIP.

AND WE ALL KNOW WHERE NICE GUYS FINISH... HEH! HEH!

THAT EVENING THE CONTESTANTS RELAX... WELL, NOT ALL OF THEM!

DEAD LAST.

AT LEAST YOU ARE NOT LAST IN THE RACE FOR LOVE.

ROCHELLE?

EXCUSE ME?

MY NAME IS FRANZ AND I AM A HUGE FAN.

I HAVE ...FANS?

44

JUST ME. I WOULD LIKE TO SAY **DANKE** FOR REPRESENTING ALL US LITTLE PLANES.

BUT YOU ARE A CAR.

JA, BUT I AM A FLUGZEUGAUTO, A FLYING CAR!

GUTEN TAG, HERR DUSTY! I AM **VON** FLIEGENHOSEN!

KLANK

DIDN'T YOU JUST SAY YOUR NAME IS FRANZ?

FRANZ IS THE GUY WHO IS IN CHARGE WHEN WE PUTTER ABOUT THE COBBLESTONES.

IN THE AIR I AM IN CHARGE!

THIS GUY NEEDS TO GET HIS HEAD GASKET CHECKED...

I HAVE A HUMBLE SUGGESTION. WOULD YOU NOT BE MUCH FASTER WITHOUT THE PIPES AND TANK?

MY SPRAYER?

JA. WHY CARRY AROUND THE EXTRA WEIGHT?

THE LITTLE CRAZY CAR IS RIGHT.

IN THE NIGHT...

THIS IS REVERSIBLE, RIGHT?

DRRIIILLL

FFRRRIGH

THE NEXT DAY...

WOOOH! THANKS FOR EVERYTHING, FRANZ... ER, VON FLIEGENHOSEN!

FANTÁSTICO!

GUTEN LUCK, HERR DUSTY!

THE RALLY CONTINUES...

IT'S OUR THIRD LEG AND WE'VE ALREADY LOST SEVERAL COMPETITORS TO EQUIPMENT FAILURE.

BUT THE REAL STORY HERE, BRENT, IS DUSTY CROPHOPPER!

AGRA AIR BASE, INDIA...

FROM LAST PLACE, ALL THE WAY TO 8TH!

OH YEAH!

MISTER RIPSLINGER, HOW CAN A CROP DUSTER OUTFLY YOU?

ONE AT A TIME!

WAIT, WHAT?

THERE HE IS!

DUSTY! DUSTY!

HOW DO YOU KEEP UP WITH THE PROS?

DUSTY, WHY DO YOU FLY SO LOW?

OH! UH! I...

WHY ARE THEY WASTING THEIR TIME WITH HIM?

ACTUALLY, IT'S A REALLY COMPELLING UNDERDOG STORY. IT'S LIKE ROCKY!

IT'S MORE LIKE DAVID AND GOLIATH!

OR OLD YELLER!

ENOUGH!

THAT FARM BOY... HE'S NOT ABOUT TO STOP ME FROM MAKING HISTORY!

WHERE DID YOU LEARN TO RACE?

FROM MY COACH, SKIPPER. HE'S AN AMAZING INSTRUCTOR AND A GREAT FRIEND.

I'M SURE IF HE COULD, HE'D BE RIGHT OUT HERE WITH US.

IF HE COULD...

VRRR VRRR

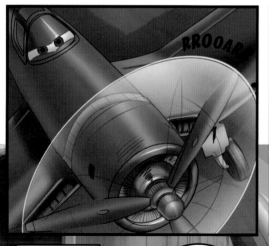

RROOAR

YOUR ENGINE SOUNDS KINDA ROUGH.

SPUTT SPUTT

MUST BE A MAG MISFIRE.

THE NEXT MORNING...

YOU GOT ANYTHING NEW?

I'M NOW SELLING THESE ONE-OF-A-KIND DUSTY COMMEMORATIVE MUGS...

47

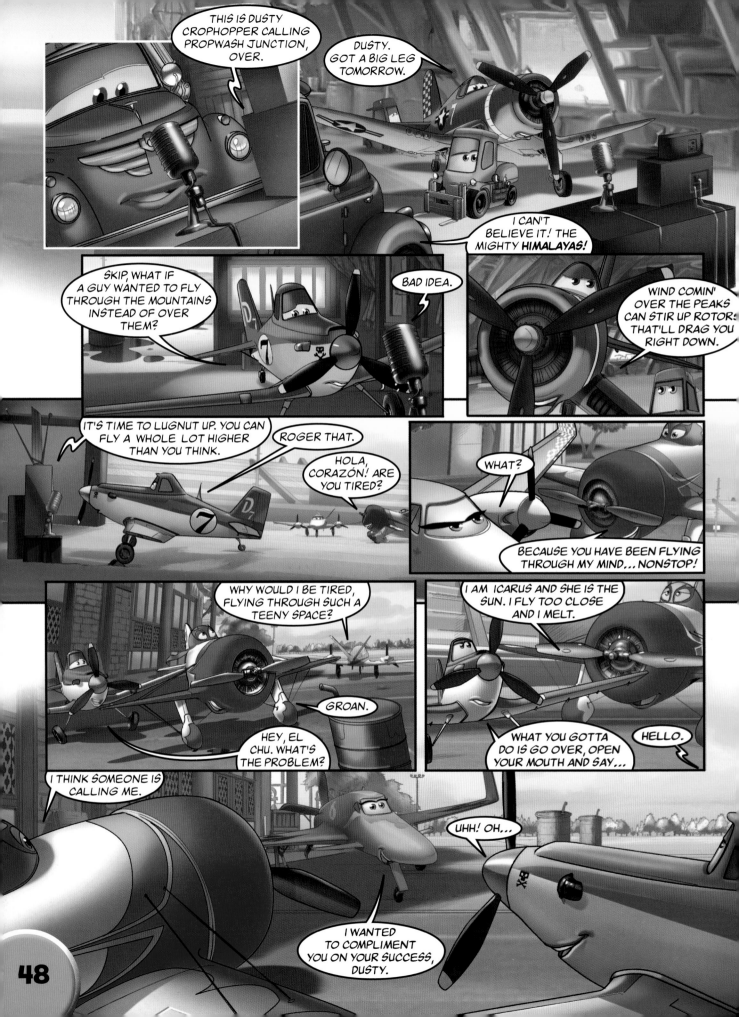

YOU ARE DOING VERY WELL FOR YOUR FIRST RACE.

THAT MEANS A LOT COMING FROM YOU. YOU ARE SO... AERODYNAMIC!

HAVE YOU EVER BEEN TO THE **TAJ MAHAL?**

NO, I HAVEN'T.

COME ON, LET'S GO.

SO...

MUST BE NICE TO BE BACK HOME.

IT'S **COMPLICATED.** I HAVE A BILLION FANS.

THEY ARE ALL EXPECTING ME TO WIN.

MAYBE THIS TIME YOU WILL.

WOW! THIS PLACE IS **AMAZING!**

AND TOMORROW YOU'LL FLY OVER THE MAGNIFICENT HIMALAYAS.

YOU LIKE TO FLY **LOW,** DON'T YOU?

THAT'S... UH... **STRATEGIC!** AIR DENSITY AND...

YOU COULD FOLLOW THE **IRON COMPASS** INSTEAD.

IT'S THE RAILROAD TRACK THROUGH A VALLEY IN THE MOUNTAINS. SO YOU CAN STILL FLY LOW.

REALLY? THANKS, ISHANI!

To be continued...

FINN McMISSILE STARTS HERE

RULES

A GAME FOR TWO PLAYERS. THE OBJECT IS TO BE THE FIRST PLAYER TO REACH HIS OR HER FINISH AREA.

How to play:
1. CHOOSE WHO WILL BE FINN AND WHO WILL BE HOLLEY.
2. TAKE TURNS ROLLING THE DIE AND MOVE YOUR TOKEN THE NUMBER OF SPACES INDICATED.
3. WHEN YOU REACH THE CENTER, MOVE ALONG ALL FOUR GEAR COLLECTION SPACES AND ROLL THE DIE ONE TIME FOR EACH SPACE. IF YOU ROLL ONE OF THE THREE NUMBERS SHOWN BELOW EACH SPACE, YOU WIN THE PIECE OF EQUIPMENT SHOWN. MARK IT ON YOUR GEAR BOARD. WHETHER YOU WIN A GEAR OR NOT, ADVANCE ONE SPACE ON YOUR NEXT TURN UNTIL YOU'VE PASSED THROUGH ALL FOUR GEAR COLLECTION SPACES.
4. AT THIS POINT, PLAYERS MOVE ALONG THEIR OWN PATHS TOWARD EITHER OF THE TWO FINISH AREAS.
5. IF YOU LAND ON A SPACE THAT REQUIRES A PIECE OF EQUIPMENT, YOU MAY PROCEED ON YOUR NEXT TURN IF YOU HAVE IT. IF YOU DO NOT HAVE IT, YOU MUST ROLL ONE OF THE THREE NUMBERS INDICATED IN ORDER TO MOVE AHEAD.

GEAR COLLECTION

2-3-4   2-3-4

HOLLEY SHIFTWELL STARTS HERE

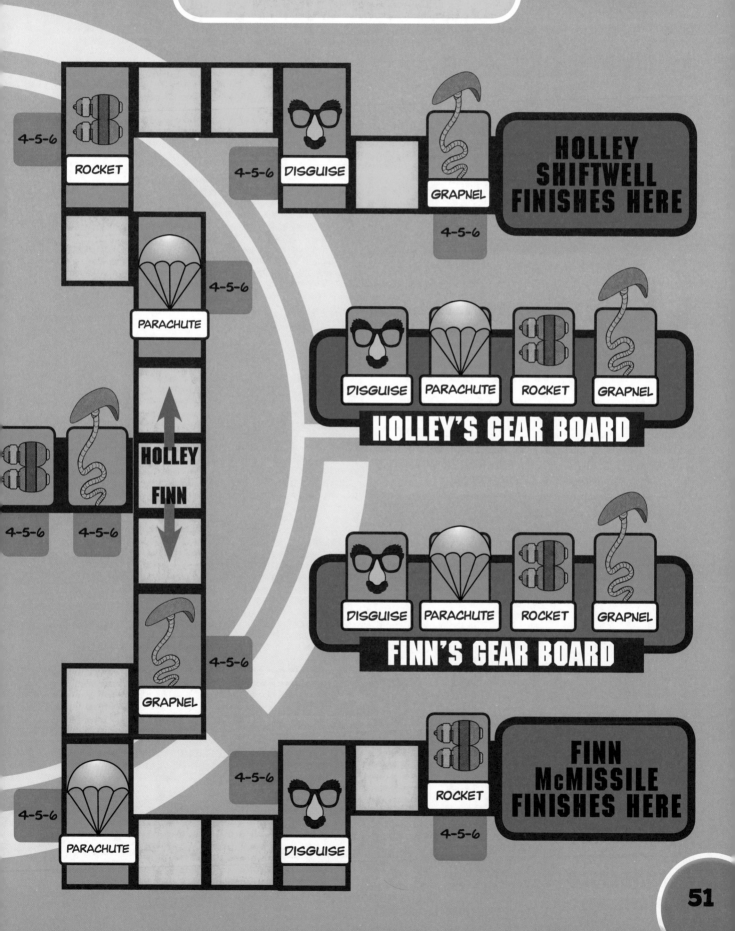

4-5-6

ROCKET

4-5-6

DISGUISE

GRAPNEL

4-5-6

HOLLEY SHIFTWELL FINISHES HERE

4-5-6

PARACHUTE

HOLLEY
FINN

4-5-6

4-5-6

DISGUISE | PARACHUTE | ROCKET | GRAPNEL

HOLLEY'S GEAR BOARD

DISGUISE | PARACHUTE | ROCKET | GRAPNEL

FINN'S GEAR BOARD

4-5-6

GRAPNEL

4-5-6

PARACHUTE

4-5-6

DISGUISE

ROCKET

FINN McMISSILE FINISHES HERE

4-5-6

DIRT & DUST

RAOUL

LIGHTNING

FRANCESCO

1

THE BEST PERFORMANCE

RAOUL, LIGHTNING, AND FRANCESCO ARE HEADED FOR AN EXCITING CHALLENGE! ADD UP THEIR SKILL POINTS (LISTED NEXT TO THIER NAMES BELOW) ON ASPHALT ●, DIRT ●, AND WET ● SURFACES. THE RACER WITH THE HIGHEST SCORE WINS!

← START

				1	2	3	4	5	6	7	TOTAL
RAOUL	1	3	2	1 +	... +	... +	... +	... +	... +	... =	...
LIGHTNING	3	2	1	3 +	... +	... +	... +	... +	... +	... =	...
FRANCESCO	3	1	2	3 +	... +	... +	... +	... +	... +	... =	...

OFF ROAD

RAOUL HAS HIT ALL THE DIRT ZONES.

COLOR THE MARKED SHAPES TO SEE THE LETTERS HE'S LEFT IN HIS PATH.

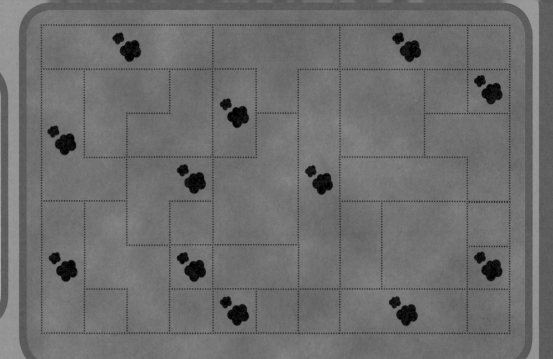

3

DIRT TREADS

EACH TIRE LEAVES A DIFFERENT TREAD MARK IN THE DIRT. COMPLETE THEM ALL BY ADDING THE CORRECT MISSING SEGMENTS.

A

B

C

D

1   2   3   4

Answers on page 171

VERY BAD OUTFIT

DISGUISE!

1

IDENTIKIT

MATER NEEDS TO DISGUISE HIMSELF AS IVAN. HELP HIM FIND IVAN'S MUSTACHE, MOUTH, HOOK, AND CLEARANCE LIGHT IN THESE COLUMNS AND WRITE THEIR CORRESPONDING LETTER BELOW. YOU WILL FIND OUT THE WORD SIGNAL MATER NEEDS TO USE.

G

H

I

J

V

X

Y

Z

Z

A

B

C

MATER

WORD SIGNAL

... ...

Answers on page 171

HOLO-MATCHING

2 HOLLEY HAS USED HER COMPUTER TO VERIFY THAT MATER CAN BE DISGUISED AS IVAN. WHICH OF THE FOUR HOLOGRAMS OF MATER MATCHES THE GREEN AREA SHOWN BELOW?

HOLLEY

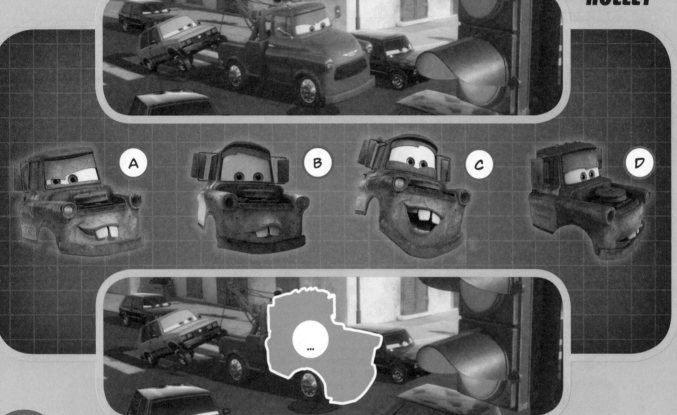

A   B   C   D

3

IVAN'S TOW-MAZE

FIND OUT WHICH OF THESE THREE CABLES IS CONNECTED TO THE HOOK THAT IVAN USES TO TOW VICTOR.

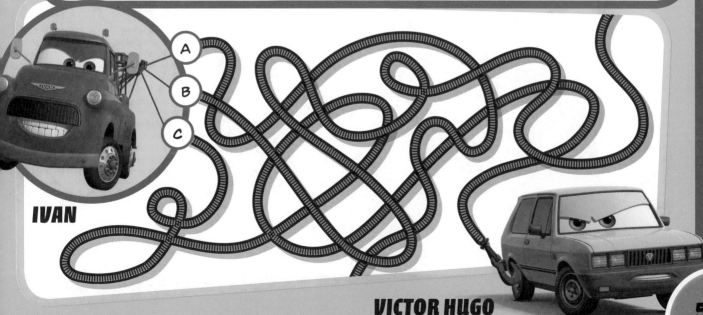

A
B
C

IVAN

VICTOR HUGO

Answers on page 171

MIRROR, MIRROR!

THE MAGIC MIRROR REFLECTS MORE THAN IT SEEMS! FIND FIVE DIFFERENCES BETWEEN THE TWO IMAGES BELOW.

SUDOKU SCRAMBLE

MICKEY, MINNIE, DONALD, AND GOOFY SHOULD APPEAR ONCE IN EACH ROW, EACH COLUMN, AND EACH OF THE FOUR LARGER SQUARES! DRAW THEM OR WRITE THEIR NAMES IN THE BLANK SQUARES.

A FULL DECK!

MICKEY'S DECK OF CARDS IS ALMOST READY FOR SHOWTIME—BUT NOT QUITE! FIND THE MISSING SHAPE TO FILL IN THE GAP ON EACH CARD. BE CAREFUL: NOT ALL OF THE SHAPES WILL FIT!

1
2
3
4
5
6
7

A
B
C
D
E

Answers on page 171

MIRROR MAZE

THIS IS NO NORMAL MAZE—YOU'LL NEED MAGIC MIRRORS TO WIN!

FOLLOW THE PATH AND TRY TO REACH THE FINISH LINE. WHEN YOU REACH A MAGIC MIRROR, YOU WILL WARP TO THE OTHER MAGIC MIRROR OF THE SAME COLOR. CONTINUE YOUR JOURNEY FROM THERE TO THE NEXT MAGIC MIRROR!

START

GO TO NEXT PAGE

CONTINUED FROM
LAST PAGE

FINISH

Answer on page 171

DINO MITE

Rex is spinning out of control. Color in Rex using the color key guide.

I CAN'T LOOK! WILL SOMEONE PLEASE COVER MY EYES?

MISSION ACCOMPLISHED!

COLOR WHEN FINISHED.

1 2 3 4 5

WOODY'S WORDS

Woody has his words mixed-up. Which of the sayings below belong to Woody? Check off the correct answer. The first one has been done for you.

YES NO

1. YOU'RE MY FAVORITE DEPUTY! ✓

PULL MY STRING!

2. WE'VE GOT A KEEPER!

3. THERE'S A SNAKE IN MY BOOT!

4. YOU'VE GOT A DATE WITH JUSTICE!

5. OOOOOOOOOOH... THE CLAW!

DID YOU KNOW?

If you pull the string on Woody's back, he always defeats villains with a witty comment or two!

MISSION ACCOMPLISHED!
COLOR WHEN FINISHED

Answers on page 172

BONNIE'S HOUSE

Playtime is never dull at Bonnie's house! Have fun solving these puzzles.

1 TEATIME TEASER

Bonnie's toys are pretending to be in a café in Paris. Look carefully at these two pictures. Can you find six things that are different in picture B?

A

B

Color in a building block as you find each difference.

Answers on page 171

GARDEN FRIENDS

The toys are playing in the yard. Draw lines to show where the missing puzzle pieces fit.

2

Which puzzle piece doesn't belong?

1 2 3
4 5 6

A

B

C

D

E

F

G

3 IT'S SHOWTIME

Mr. Pricklepants is acting. Which picture of him is the odd one out?

The answer is:

A B C D

WHO ARE YOU CALLING PEABRAIN?

MISSION ACCOMPLISHED!

COLOR WHEN FINISHED.

Answers on page 171

EL CHU IS POSING FOR YOU! **ADD SOME COLORS** TO THIS SCENE! TAKE INSPIRATION FROM THE OPPOSITE PAGE FOR THE **CHARACTER,** AND LET YOUR IMAGINATION RUN WILD FOR THE **BACKGROUND!**

EL CHUPACABRA

SUDOKU PUZZLE

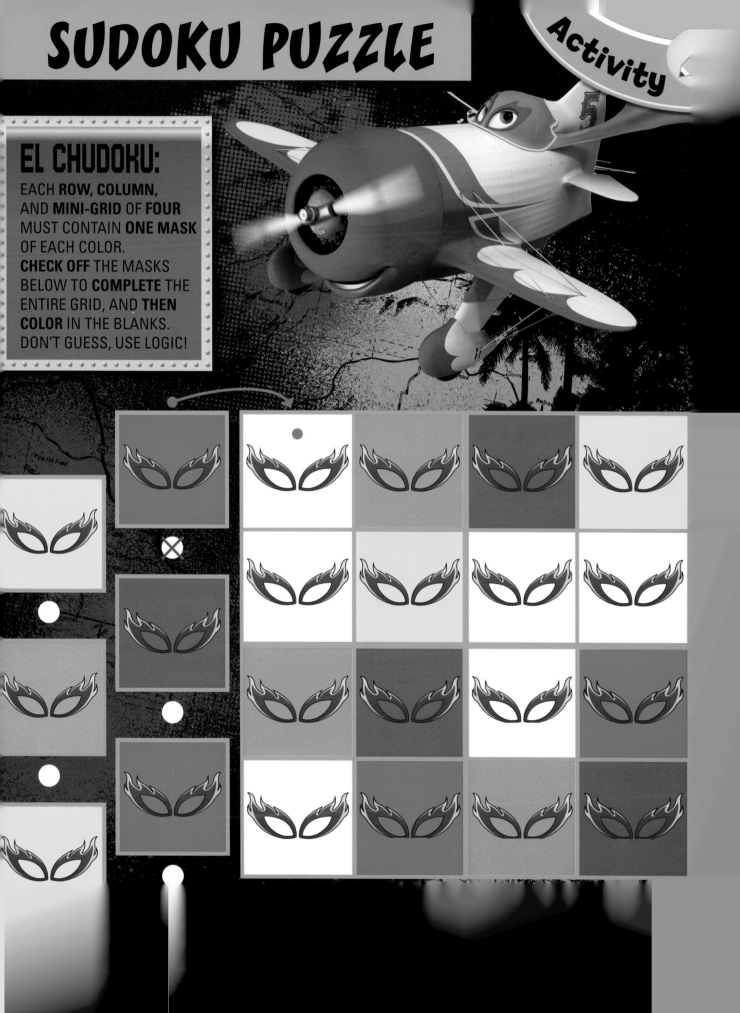

Activity

EL CHUDOKU:

EACH **ROW, COLUMN,** AND **MINI-GRID** OF **FOUR** MUST CONTAIN **ONE MASK** OF EACH COLOR. **CHECK OFF** THE MASKS BELOW TO **COMPLETE** THE ENTIRE GRID, AND **THEN COLOR** IN THE BLANKS. DON'T GUESS, USE LOGIC!

ANYTIME.

REALLY GOOD ADVICE...

EVERY RACER'S NIGHTMARE IS SCALING THE HIMALAYAS.

IT'S A SHORT LEG AHEAD, BUT EXTREMELY TREACHEROUS!

WHOA!

SCRAAAATCH

TOOOOOOT

SCREEEEEEECH

VROOOOOM

AND AFTER ALL THAT SMOKE...

HELLO? IS THIS WHERE I'M SUPPOSED TO BE?

THAT IS ONE OF LIFE'S GREAT QUESTIONS.

GASP! I'M DEAD!

MR. CROPHOPPER. WELCOME TO NEPAL.

PHEEEW! HAVE THE OTHERS LEFT ALREADY?

ACTUALLY, NO ONE ELSE IS HERE YET. YOU'RE IN FIRST PLACE!

THAT EVENING...

HE FLEW THROUGH A WHAT?

A TUNNEL?

THAT IS CRAZY!

SÍ, CRAZY LIKE A FIREFOX!

RIGHT HERE! COME ON!

HOW DOES IT FEEL TO BE IN FIRST PLACE?

IT FEELS GREAT. BUT MORE THAN ANYTHING, I'M HAPPY I FIT THROUGH THAT TUNNEL.

EXCUSE ME, GUYS.

CRAZY DAY TODAY, HUH?

YEAH. A VERY EXCITING WIN FOR YOU.

HEY, YOUR PROPELLER? IT'S NEW-SKYSLICER MARK FIVE, RIGHT?

AREN'T THOSE MADE EXCLUSIVELY **FOR RIPSLINGER'S RACE TEAM?**

DUSTY, I...

I REALLY THOUGHT THAT YOU'D JUST TURN AROUND.

WELL, YOU WERE WRONG. AND I WAS WRONG ABOUT YOU.

OH HEY, RIP. THANKS FOR FIRST PLACE.

CENTRAL CHINA...

FLYING LOW AND QUICK, DUSTY CROPHOPPER IS MANAGING TO HOLD ON TO THE TOP SPOT.

BUT CURRENT REIGNING CHAMP RIPSLINGER IS JUST SECONDS BEHIND HIM!

SHANGHAI PUDONG INTERNATIONAL AIRPORT...

WE HEAD OUT ACROSS THE PACIFIC TOMORROW, SKIP.

YOU WERE STATIONED THERE FOR A WHILE. GOT ANY ADVICE?

BE CAREFUL.

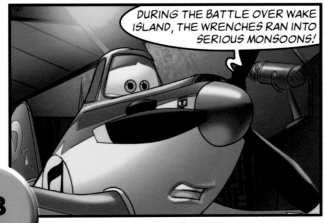

DURING THE BATTLE OVER WAKE ISLAND, THE WRENCHES RAN INTO SERIOUS MONSOONS!

AND ONE MORE THING...

...I'M **PROUD** OF YOU, DUSTY.

THANKS... "WINGMAN."

HEY, DUSTY, WE HAVE A SURPRISE FOR YOU!

WE'RE GONNA MEET YOU IN **MEXICO**! TICKETS ARE ON SPARKY AND ME!

WE SOLD 326 DUSTY BOBBLEHEADS, 143 ANTENNA BALLS, 203 SPINNER MUGS...

... AND ONE THOUSAND WHISTLES! GO TEAM DUSTERINO!

LATER THAT NIGHT...

CLICK

LOVE MACHINE!!!

NO! NO! NO! A THOUSAND **NOS**!

SLAM

SOB!

QUÉ PASA? DUSTY, WHAT ARE YOU DOING?

CLICK

LOW AND SLOW.

TCHICA TCHICA

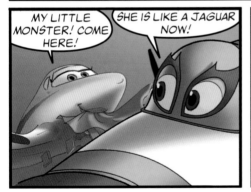

BOGY IS A CIVILIAN. EMERGENCY FUEL.

COPY THAT.

THAT'S ALL I NEED, A CIVILIAN **EXPLODING** ON MY DECK!

WE COULD RIG THE BARRICADE, SIR.

ALL YOU GOTTA DO IS END UP IN THE **SPAGHETTI**.

I'M NOT SURE I CAN DO THIS! THAT RUNWAY IS **MOVING**!

SPROOOOING

WHOOOAAA!

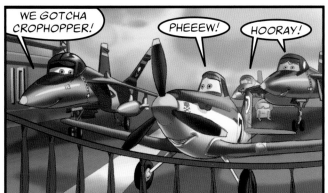

WE GOTCHA CROPHOPPER!

PHEEEW!

HOORAY!

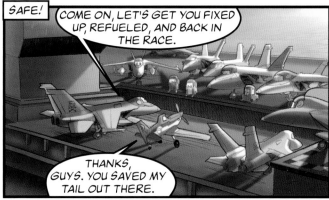

SAFE!

COME ON, LET'S GET YOU FIXED UP, REFUELED, AND BACK IN THE RACE.

THANKS, GUYS. YOU SAVED MY TAIL OUT THERE.

HEY, WHAT IS THAT?

THAT'S THE **JOLLY WRENCHES** WALL OF FAME!

EVERY FLYER, EVERY MISSION.

SKIPPER... THERE HE IS! **BUT**...

...WHY'S THERE ONLY **ONE** MISSION?

GLENDAL CANAL

MEANWHILE...

CHUG. WHAT'S ALL THAT?

I'VE NEVER BEEN OUT OF THE COUNTRY. GOTTA BE PREPARED, RIGHT?

SKIPPER?

COME IN, SKIPPER!

DUSTY? WE'RE HEADIN' OFF TO MEXICO RIGHT NOW!

I SAW THE WALL OF FAME... THEY ONLY LIST ONE MISSION FOR YOU.

GLAD YA GOT THERE SAFE. WEATHER REPORT SAYS A MAJOR STORM BREWIN' OUT THERE.

I'M NOT IN MEXICO. I'M WITH THE JOLLY WRENCHES.

YOU'RE ON THE FLYSENHOWER?

IT MUST BE A MISTAKE...

LOOK YOU'VE GOTTA GET OUTTA THERE! YOU'RE GONNA HAVE TO **FLY HIGH**!

IS IT TRUE?

LISTEN TO ME, GET ABOVE THE STORM...

SKIPPER! IS IT **TRUE**?

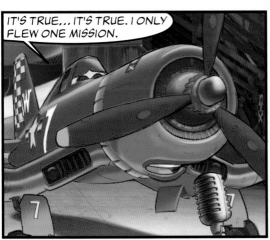

IT'S TRUE... IT'S TRUE. I ONLY FLEW ONE MISSION.

BUT ALL THOSE STORIES...

CROPHOPPER! WE'VE GOT WEATHER MOVING IN FAST.

ON DECK...

THE CAT WILL TAKE YA FROM ZERO TO 160 KNOTS IN **TWO SECONDS.**

YOU'VE GOT TO TAKE OFF! YOU DON'T GO NOW, YOU DON'T GO **AT ALL.**

ENGINE FULL THROTTLE, NOD TO THE SHOOTER WHEN YOU'RE SET.

GO WIN IT FOR THE WRENCHES, DUSTY! **VOLO PRO VERITAS!**

GO!

CLANK WOOOOSH

MEXICO INTERNATIONAL AIRPORT...

SEÑOR RIPSLINGER, DO YOU HAVE ANY COMMENTS ON THE DISAPPEARANCE OF DUSTY CROPHOPPER?

DUSTY WAS A NICE GUY.

HE FLEW THE CHALLENGE AND PIERCED THE CLOUDS OF MEDIOCRITY. EXCUSE ME.

LET'S HOPE HE MAKES A BETTER BOAT THAN A PLANE.

THAT WAS A GOOD ONE, BOSS.

MALVADO! SEÑOR DUSTY HAS TEN TIMES THE ENGINE YOU DO!

AND TEN TIMES THE **INTEGRITY!**

SAID THE PLANE WITH THE SHINY NEW PROPELLER...

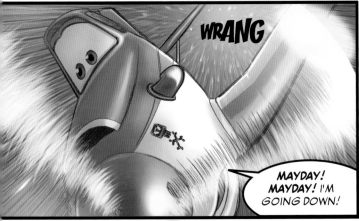

JUST IN TIME...

QUICK, TO THE HANGAR!

DUSTY!

BROKEN WING RIBS, TWISTED GEAR, BENT PROP, AND YOUR MAIN SPAR IS CRACKED...

IT'S OVER.

ONE MISSION? SO MUCH FOR "VOLO PRO VERITAS".

CAN WE GET A MINUTE ALONE, PLEASE?

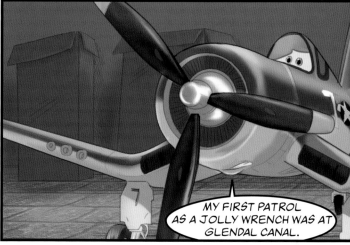

MY FIRST PATROL AS A JOLLY WRENCH WAS AT GLENDAL CANAL.

"MY SQUADRON WAS ALL ROOKIES... I TRAINED EVERY SINGLE ONE OF 'EM..."

LOOK, SKIPPER. ENEMY SHIP, TWO O'CLOCK LOW.

NEGATIVE, JIGSAW 2. OUR ORDERS ARE TO RECON AND REPORT BACK.

COME ON SKIP, IT'LL BE A TURKEY SHOOT!

VROOOAAAM

ALL RIGHT. LET'S GO IN FOR A CLOSER LOOK.

"IT WAS TOO LATE TO PULL UP..."

HOLY COW! IT'S THE WHOLE ENEMY FLEET!

AAGH!

BLAM

JIGSAW 2!

RAT-TAT-TAT

UUNGH!

BOOM

"MY WHOLE SQUADRON... UNDER MY COMMAND... GONE."

AFTER THAT I JUST COULDN'T BRING MYSELF TO FLY AGAIN.

IF YOU KNEW THE TRUTH ABOUT MY PAST, WOULD YOU HAVE ASKED ME TO TRAIN YOU?

I'M SORRY, DUSTY.

77

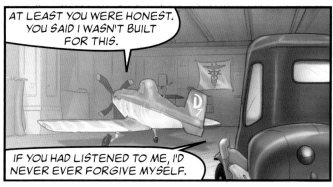

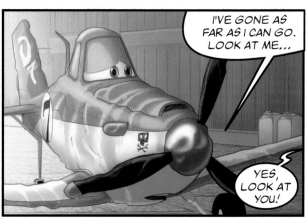

BUT WITH **MY OLD** PROPELLER. THIS ONE DIDN'T REALLY SUIT ME.

I THINK YOU WILL HAVE A LOT BETTER LUCK WITH IT.

THANKS, ISHANI! DOTTIE, CAN YOU FIX ME?

DOES A **P-T-SIX-A** HAVE A MULTISTAGE COMPRESSOR?

"YES. IT DOES!"

THERE'S A LOT OF WORK TO DO...

... BUT THERE'S ALSO TIME TO **STUDY THE OPPONENT!**

WHEN THE MORNING COMES...

WHOA... DUDE.

WE'LL SEE YOU IN NEW YORK!

HA! IT'S DUSTIN' TIME!

DUSTY!

HE'S BACK!

WHOA, WHO'S THAT GUY?

IT'S THE CROP DUSTER!

ANOTHER ONE?

IT'S THE SAME ONE, KNUCKLEHEAD!

BOLTING ON A FEW NEW PARTS DOESN'T CHANGE WHO YOU ARE.

YOU'RE AFRAID OF GETTING BEAT BY A CROP DUSTER.

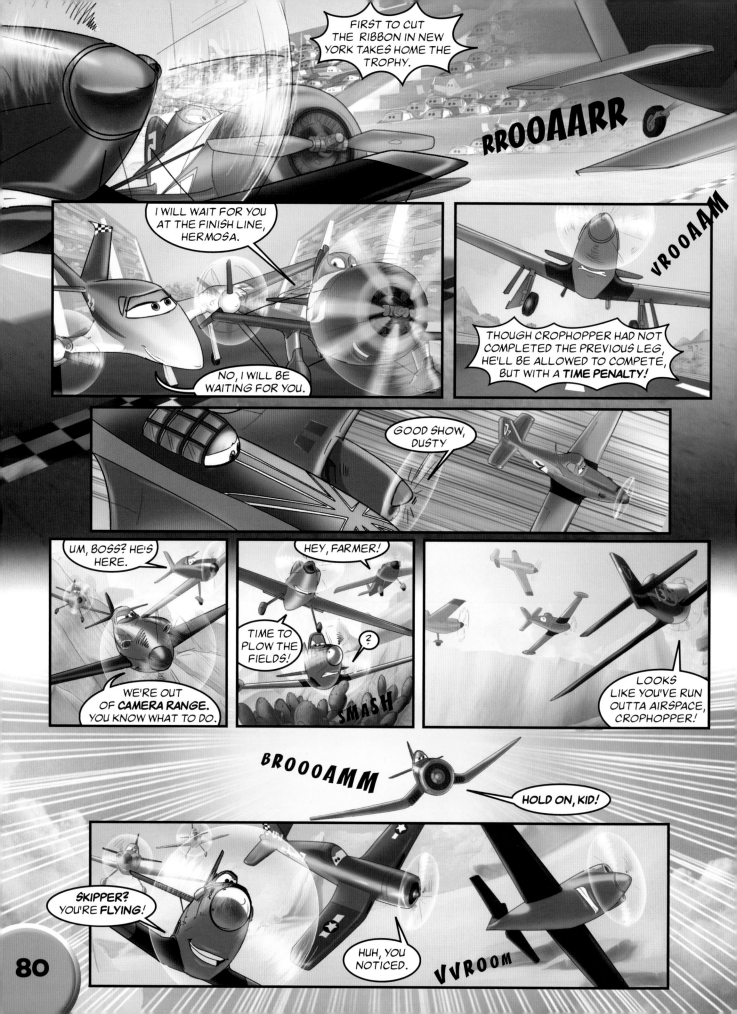

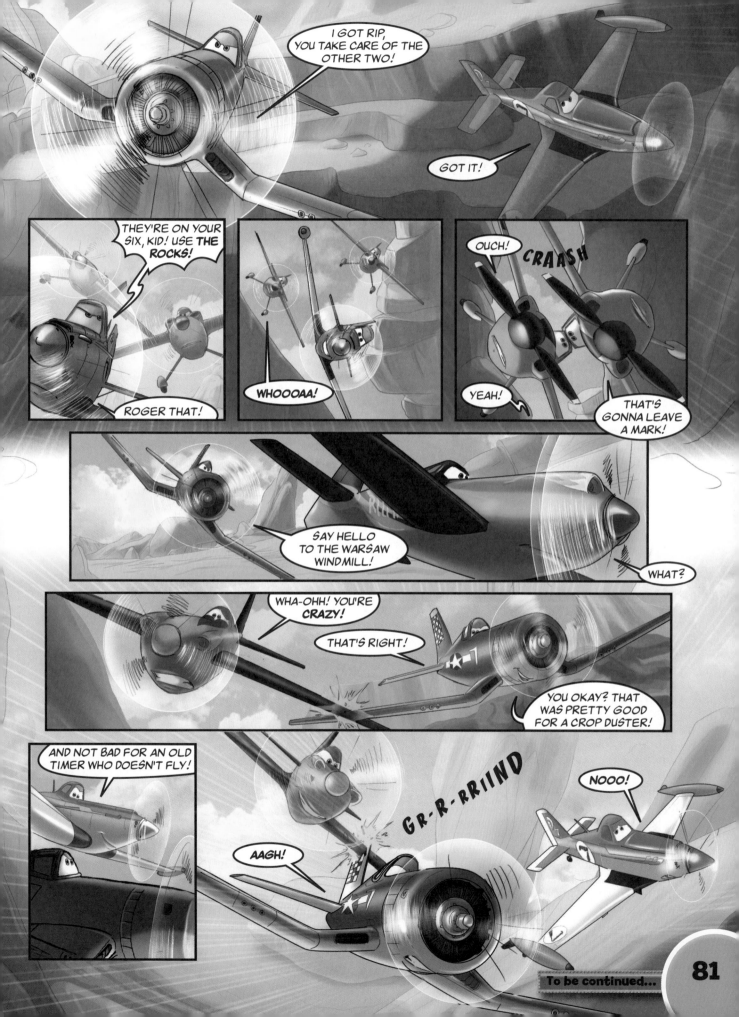

To be continued...

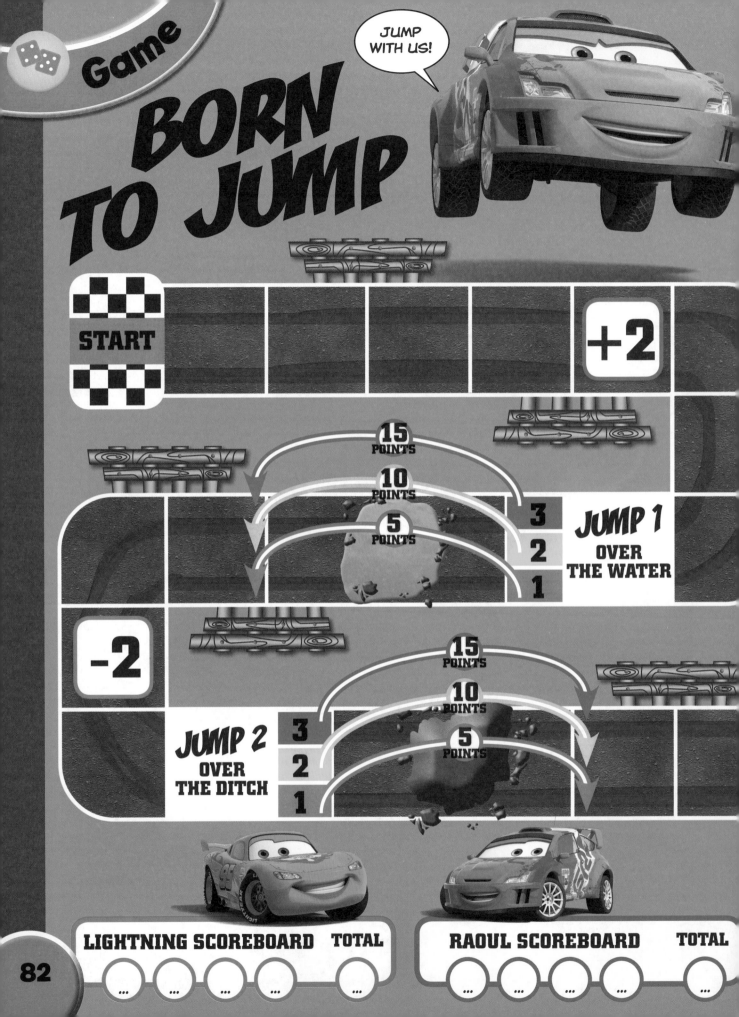

How to play:

1. CHOOSE WHO WILL BE LIGHTNING AND WHO WILL BE RAOUL.
2. PUT THE TOKENS AT THE START. TAKE TURNS ROLLING THE DIE AND MOVING THE NUMBER OF SPACES INDICATED.
3. FOLLOW THE INSTRUCTIONS ON THE PLUS/MINUS SPACES. STOP WHEN YOU COME TO A JUMP SPACE, EVEN IF YOUR ROLL OF THE DIE INDICATES THAT YOU CAN MOVE FARTHER.
4. ROLL AGAIN TO JUMP. THE NUMBER YOU ROLL EARNS THE NUMBER OF POINTS SHOWN.
5. WRITE THEM ON YOUR SCOREBOARD AND ADD THEM UP AT THE END OF THE RACE.

THE FIRST PLAYER TO CROSS THE FINISH LINE WINS THE RACE.
THE PLAYER WITH THE HIGHEST SCORE IS CHAMPION JUMPER!

JUMP 3 OVER THE DUST CLOUD — 3, 2, 1 — 15 POINTS / 10 POINTS / 5 POINTS

JUMP 4 OVER THE LOGS — 3, 2, 1 — 15 POINTS / 10 POINTS / 5 POINTS

MUD PUDDLE MISS 1 TURN

1

+1

FINISH

A RIBBON FOR THE WINNER!

I'M FIRST!

YOU'LL NEED:

TIP:
ASK AN ADULT TO HELP YOU!

• 3 PIECES OF CARDBOARD (WHITE, BLUE, AND RED) • 1 PENCIL • 1 CUP • 1 PLATE • 1 BOTTLE CAP • SAFETY SCISSORS • GLUE

1 DRAW 3 OUTLINES: THE BOTTOM OF A CUP ON RED CARDBOARD, A PLATE ON BLUE CARDBOARD, A CAP ON WHITE CARDBOARD.

2 CUT OUT THE DISKS AND GLUE THEM ON TOP OF ONE ANOTHER, AS SHOWN.

GLUE

3 CUT OUT TINY TRIANGLES ALONG THE EDGE OF THE BLUE DISK (THE LARGEST). CUT ONLY AS FAR AS THE RED EDGE, AND NO FARTHER.

4 CUT 2 STRIPS FROM THE REMAINING CARDBOARD, THE WIDTH OF YOUR CAP. CUT OUT A TRIANGLE FROM ONE END OF EACH STRIP, AS SHOWN.

5 GLUE THE TWO COLORED STRIPS TO THE BACK OF THE DISKS, ONE SLANTING TO THE LEFT, THE OTHER TO THE RIGHT.

GLUE

GLUE

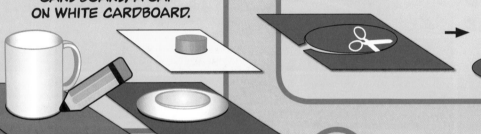

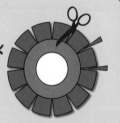

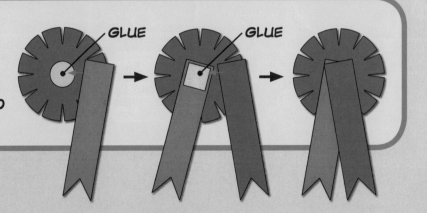

6 COMPLETE YOUR RIBBON BY WRITING YOUR POSITION NUMBER ON CARDBOARD AND GLUING IT IN THE CENTER.

1ST

GLUE

TIP:

MAKE OTHER RIBBONS AND AWARD THEM TO YOUR FRIENDS!

1st

YOUR RIBBON IS READY!

PLAY WITH FILLMORE

1 SLURP!

FILLMORE AND SARGE ENJOY SOME TASTY OIL IN CARSOLI. PUT THE JUMBLED BOTTOM SCENE IN ORDER. WRITE THE LETTERS FROM THE TOP BENEATH THE CORRECT NUMBERED SEGMENTS.

A B C D E F G H I

1 2 3 4 5 6 7 8 9

C ... ...

2 **A WELL-STOCKED SUPPLY**

FILLMORE'S GOT LOTS OF EXTRA FUEL CANS.
FIND THE MATCHING PAIRS AND CIRCLE THEM!

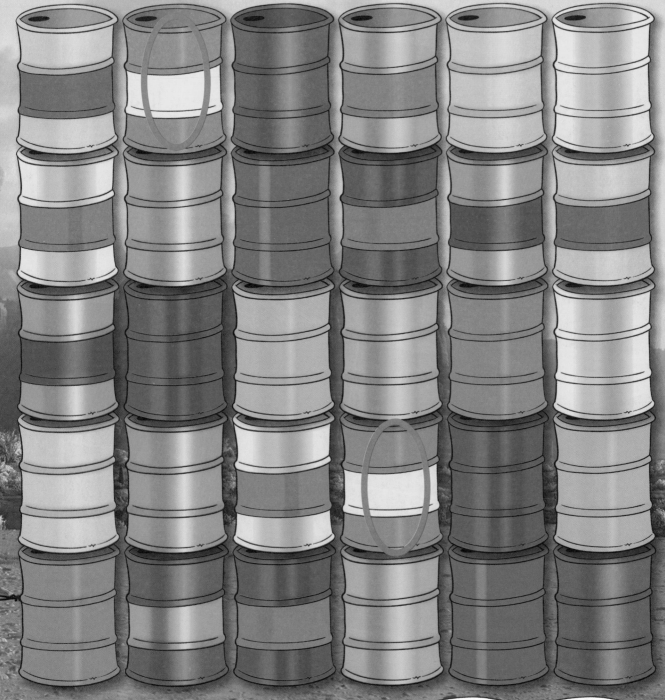

3 **FIND AND COLOR**

TWO CANS HAVE NO MATCH.
FIND THEM AND PUT AN X
THROUGH EACH ONE. THEN
COLOR THESE TWO BLANK CANS
TO MATCH THE ODD CANS!

Answers on page 172

HAWAIIAN VACATION

The toys are creating a pretend vacation for Barbie and Ken. Kick back and relax with this puzzle.

Can you find and circle six differences in the bottom picture? There's one difference in each square.

WELCOME TO PARADISE!

MISSION ACCOMPLISHED!

COLOR WHEN FINISHED.

88   Answers on page 172

PUZZLES MISSION

Buzz is embarking on a dangerous mission. Help him fight the forces of evil by completing these puzzles.

1 Buzz must cross the floating disks to defeat Zurg. What message is written in green?

EVIL WILL BE DEFEATED!

F
A
T
M
H
G
I
B
START
F

2 Color in the odd planet out.

A   B   C   D   E

Answers on page 172

PREPARE for doom, BUZZ LIGHTYEAR!

R
N
X
D
F
L
I
S
G
H
T

FINISH

MISSION ACCOMPLISHED!

COLOR WHEN FINISHED.

3 Circle the two Aliens that are exactly the same.

A   B   C

4 Is there an ODD number or EVEN number of meteorites?

Answers on page 172

OPERATION PLAYTIME ①

Woody wants to make sure that all the toys in the toy box get played with. Solve these teasers and let playtime begin...

DOODLING FUN
Woody has challenged Etch A Sketch® to a dual. Add up these sums below to see who has finished the most drawings?

WOODY: 5 + 4 + 2 + 1 = _____

ETCH A SKETCH®: 1 + 2 + 8 + 4 = _____

② TINY TOYS
Can you put the family of Troikas in height order, starting with the shortest first?

A   B   C   D   E

The correct order is: _D_ __ __ __ __

3

SPELL IT OUT
Can you help Mr. Spell unscramble the letters to make a mystery word? We have entered the first letter for you.

LPAYTEIM

P _ _ _ _ _ _ _

ME HELP WOODY!

4

MR. MUSCLE
Rocky Gibraltar is the strongest toy in the toy box, but there's someone he can't lift. Look at the close-ups. Who is it?

L _ _ _ _ _

MISSION ACCOMPLISHED!

COLOR WHEN FINISHED.

Answers on page 172

LANDING STRIPS

1 IN FOR A LANDING: OUR FRIENDS NEED TO FIND THE RIGHT ROUTE FOR THEIR LANDINGS NUMBERED 1 TO 4. HELP THEM FOLLOW THE PATHS THAT SPELL THEIR NAMES.

BRAVO

DUSTY CROPHOPPER

RIPSLINGER

EL CHUPACABRA

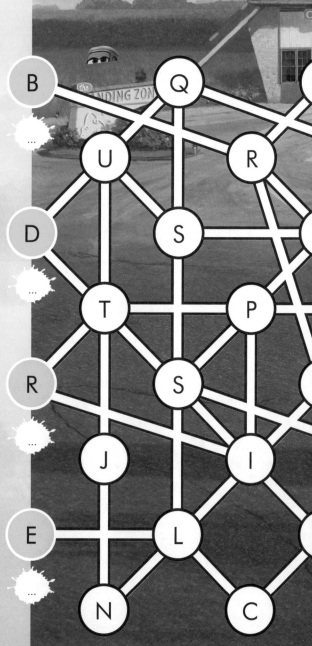

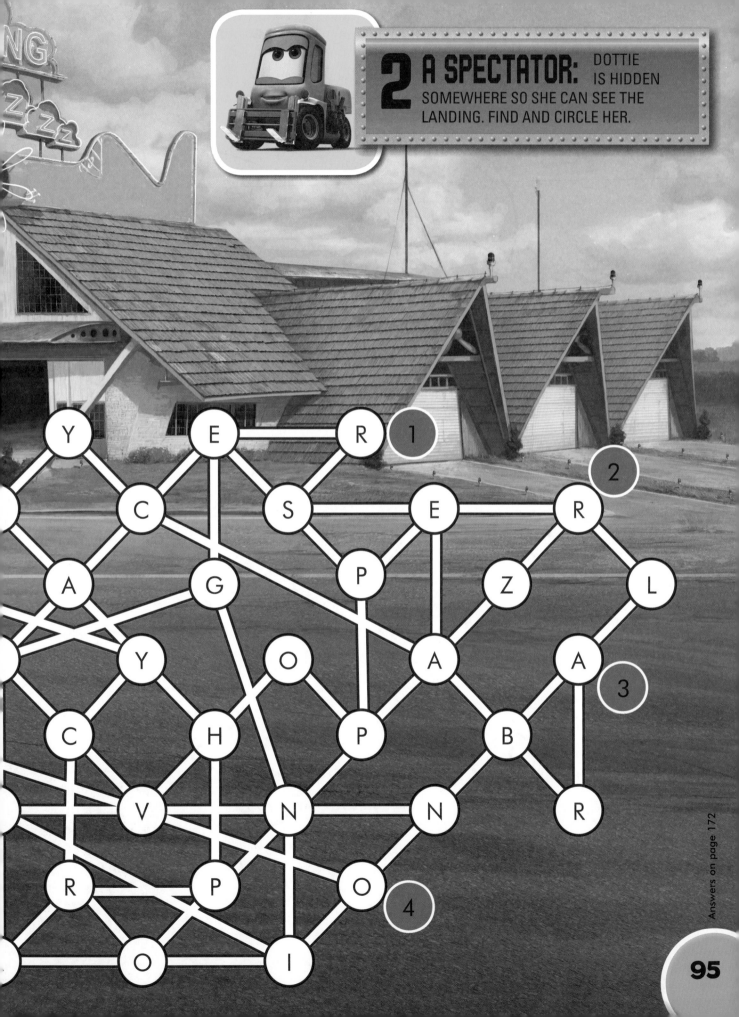

Y E R 1

2

C S E R

A G P Z L

Y O A A 3

C H P B

V N N R

R P O 4

O I

Answers on page 172

RESCUE MISSION

1 MAYDAY, MAYDAY: DUSTY'S SENT OUT AN **S.O.S.** AND NEEDS HELP FAST. AMONG THE **35** RADAR SCREENS BELOW, THE ONLY ONE **WITHOUT A MATCH** IS THE ONE THAT SHOWS **HIS POSITION.** FIND IT!

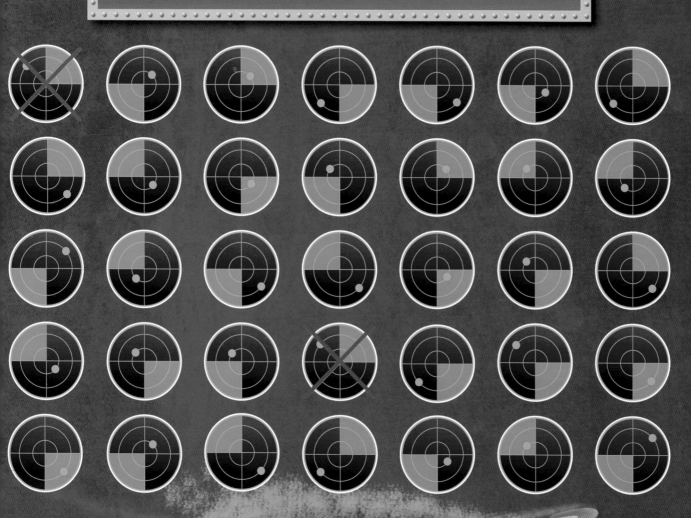

Answers on page 172

THAT IS WHY THEY CALL 'EM SKYSLICERS!

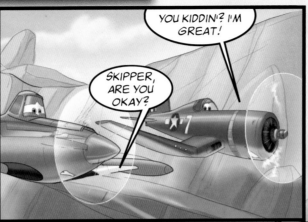

SKIPPER, ARE YOU OKAY?

YOU KIDDIN'? I'M GREAT!

GO GET HIM! GO!

OVER THE MISSISSIPPI RIVER...

WE'RE CLOSING IN ON THE FINAL STRETCH, FOLKS!

THAT'S RIGHT, COLIN, AND RIPSLINGER HAS MAINTAINED A FORMIDABLE LEAD!

HI!

WHAT?

ARRGH! NO, NO, NOOO!

WOOOSH

"TAILWINDS LIKE NOTHING YOU'VE EVER FLOWN..."

ROGER THAT SKIP!

DON'T LOOK DOWN! DON'T LOOK DOWN!

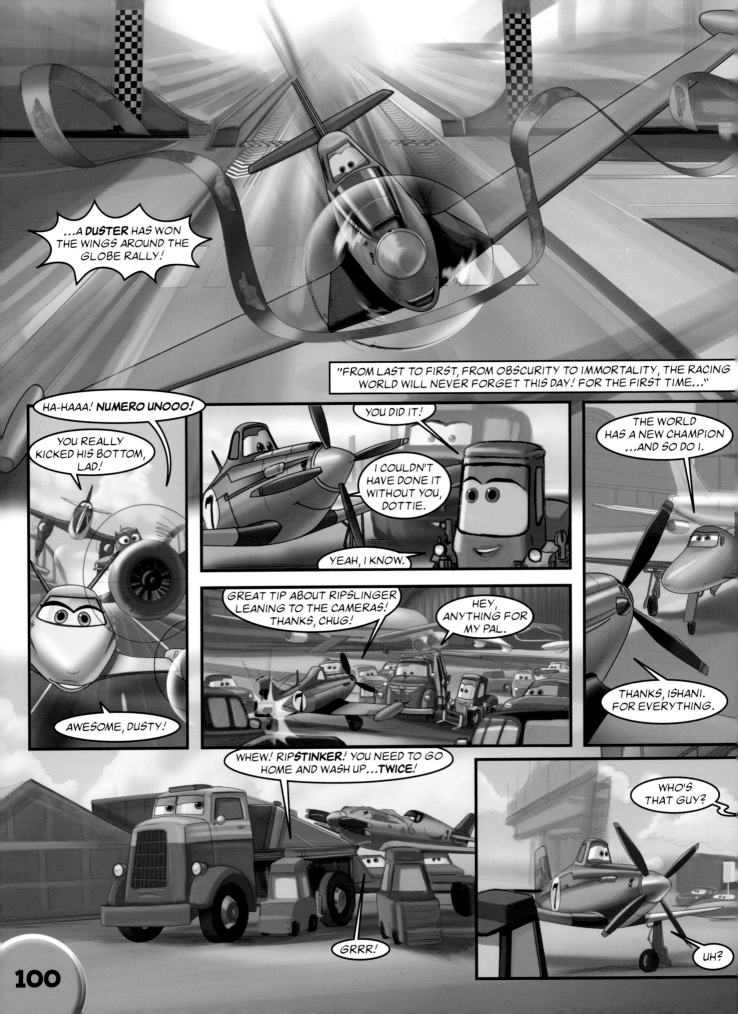

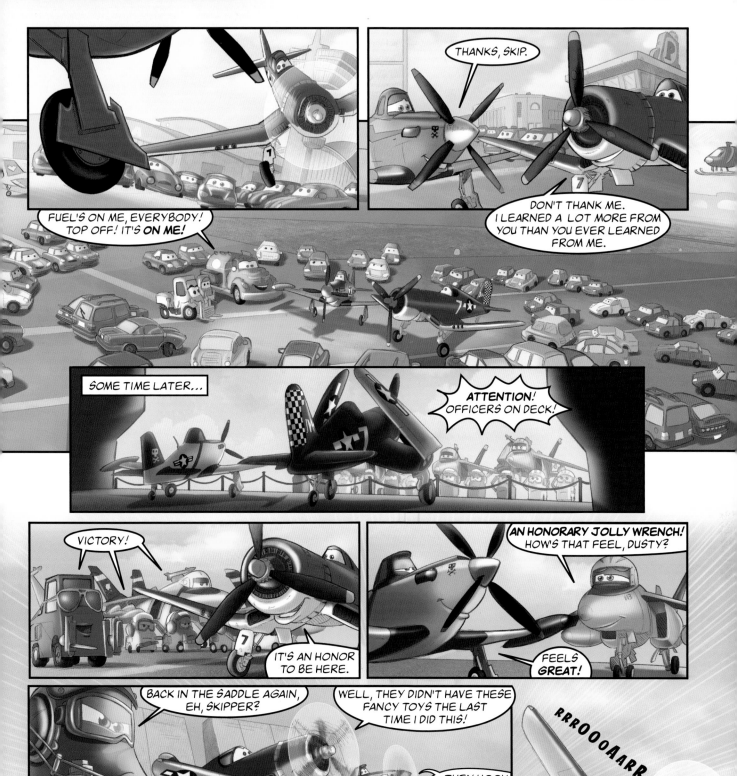

FUEL'S ON ME, EVERYBODY! TOP OFF! IT'S **ON ME!**

THANKS, SKIP.

DON'T THANK ME. I LEARNED A LOT MORE FROM YOU THAN YOU EVER LEARNED FROM ME.

SOME TIME LATER...

ATTENTION! OFFICERS ON DECK!

VICTORY!

IT'S AN HONOR TO BE HERE.

AN HONORARY JOLLY WRENCH! HOW'S THAT FEEL, DUSTY?

FEELS GREAT!

BACK IN THE SADDLE AGAIN, EH, SKIPPER?

WELL, THEY DIDN'T HAVE THESE FANCY TOYS THE LAST TIME I DID THIS!

THEY HOOK YA UP, YOU NOD TO THE SHOOTER OVER THERE...

...AND **HANG ON!** LAST ONE BACK TO PROPWASH BUYS!

RRROOOAARR

FWOOOSH

YEEEAH-HEAH! YOU'RE ON!

THE END

MATER'S SPECIALTY!

RADIATOR SPRINGS, A DAY LIKE ANY OTHER... MORE OR LESS!

HERE IT IS

HEY! WHERE DID ALL THESE CARS COME FROM?

AND MORE IMPORTANTLY... WHERE ARE THEY GOING?

DIDN'T MATER TELL YOU?

TELL ME WHAT?

BRIC-A-BRAC
TRINKETS
SALE DAY ONLY

TODAY'S THE GRAND OPENING OF HIS NEW STORE!

THIS IS LIKE HOODSTOCK, MAN!

MATER HAS A STORE?! WHAT DOES HE SELL?

MATER'S COLLECTIBLES

now open

←IN

WELCOME TO MATER'S, INTERNATIONAL ACCESSORIES SHOP!

MINIVANS! SUPERMINIS! FAMILY AND SPORTS VEHICLES! CUSTOM ACCESSORIES FOR ALL TASTES!

HOWDY! I WANT THIS!

GREAT, PAL! YOU KNOW WHO GAVE ME THIS?

MY BUDDY ZEN MASTER! A REAL TOUGH GUY!

I WAS AT THE WORLD GRAND PRIX PARTY WITH MY BEST FRIEND, LIGHTNING McQUEEN, WHEN...

...I TOLD HIM HE DID A GOOD JOB— TOOK OFF ALL THE LEAVES!

GREAT STORY, MATER!

THANKS!

Y'ALL COME BACK NOW, GEORGE!

I WANT THIS!

EXCELLENT CHOICE! IT'S ALL THE WAY FROM PARIS! I WAS THERE, TOO, WITH MY GIRL AND A SECRET AGENT!

I'D JUST ARRIVED AT THE AIRPORT WHEN...

AND CUSTOMER AFTER CUSTOMER...

...STORY AFTER STORY...

PORTO CORSA, ITALY! YOU GOTTA GO THERE, FRANCIS! AT FIRST SIGHT, I COULDN'T BELIEVE IT...

...AT LAST, DAY'S END!

SO, HOW'D THE FIRST DAY GO?

MATER'S COLLECTIBLES

CLOSED!

THE SECRET OF DRACUDUCK!

J-2765-2

DONALD DUCK AND FETHRY DUCK HAVE BEEN HIRED AS DUCKDINI THE MAGICIAN'S ASSISTANT. DUCKDINI IS PREPARING A SHOW FOR SCROOGE TV. UNFORTUNATELY, A SPELL HAS TURNED DUCKDINI INTO A BIG COWARD AND THE COURAGE POTION IS GUARDED IN DRACUDUCK THE VAMPIRE'S CASTLE!

THIS WAY, PLEASE! THE **TOUR** CONTINUES IN THE KITCHENS!

KITCHEN

107

DRACUDUCK THE VAMPIRE'S CASTLE! THIS PLACE OOZES HORROR...I STILL CAN'T BELIEVE I'M **INSIDE THESE WALLS!**

CLIC

N-NEITHER CAN I... **BRRR...**C-CAN'T WE GET OUT OF HERE?

AFTER **COMING ALL** THIS WAY? FORGET ABOUT IT!

AND ANYWAY, ALL THE MONSTERS HAVE GOT TO BE **JUST AN ACT** FOR THE TOURISTS! HAVE A LITTLE **COURAGE!**

C-COURAGE IS EXACTLY WHAT WE CAME **TO GET...**

AND **WE'LL FIND** IT SOON! LOOK, THERE'S **THE LIBRARY!**

LIBRARY

COME ON IF THERE'S ANY PLACE WE'LL FIND THE BOOK WITH THE COURAGE POTION, IT'S BEHIND THIS DOOR!

LIBRARY

STOP!

ENT-RANCE FOR-BIDDEN! YOU CAN-NOT GO IN!

BUT WE...*UM*... WE'RE **SCHOLARS** LOOKING FOR RARE BOOKS!

THE **TOWN JUNK-YARD** HAS A TON OF OLD BO-OKS! GO LO-OK THERE!

?!

LOOK, DONALD! A PHOTO WITH FRANKENSTEIN'S MONSTER! ALL THE MEMBERS OF THE **FRIENDS OF THE DISGRACED SOCIETY** WILL BE SO JEALOUS OF ME!

SNORT!

WOULD YOU STOP MESSING AROUND WITH THAT **PHONE?** WE HAVE TO FIND A WAY TO GET INTO THE LIBRARY OR WE'LL NEVER CURE DUCKDINI!

WELL, WHAT'S THE PROBLEM? **WE'LL HIDE IN THE CASTLE** UNTIL TONIGHT, AND WHEN SECURITY LEAVES WE CAN MAKE OUR MOVE UNDISTURBED! EASY, HUH?

GASP! FETHRY, SOMETIMES YOUR **CUNNING** SHOCKS ME!

FOR A LONG TIME NOW WE'VE BEEN HELPING OUR MASTER WITH HIS **NOBLE** WORK...

...STOPPING THE **EVIL CREATURES** OF THIS REGION FROM GOING OUT INTO THE WORLD!

A WHILE AGO, DRACUDUCK TOLD US THAT HE HAD TO PREPARE HIMSELF TO FACE A TERRIBLE ENEMY. THEN HE SHUT HIMSELF IN THE LIBRARY, ORDERING US NOT TO DISTURB HIM!

HE HASN'T COME OUT SINCE! BUT HE WAS THE ONE WHO **PAID US,** SO WHEN WE **ENDED UP SHORT** ON CASH...

...WE GOT THE IDEA TO OPEN THE CASTLE TO TOURISTS TO GET A BIT OF MONEY!

HOW LONG HAS DRACUDUCK BEEN SHUT IN THE LIBRARY?

TWO HUNDRED YEARS!

GIVE OR TAKE A MONTH!

To be continued...

1

Watch Out!
Do you think you are tough enough to add some color to Woody and Buzz to help them escape?

3

How many dinosaurs can you count?

Answers on page 172

FACE OFF

Mr. Potato Head has just been played with and he is missing all his facial parts.

Can you help the toys put Mr. Potato Head back together again by drawing in the missing parts, then coloring him in?

We have done the first one for you.

I'M ALL MASHED UP!

MISSION ACCOMPLISHED!

COLOR WHEN FINISHED.

Mr. Potato Head® © Hasbro, Inc.

TIDY FUN

RC, Woody, and Buzz are trying to make tidying up into a fun game. Can you find the things below in the picture? Check the box as you spot each object.

MISSION ACCOMPLISHED!

COLOR WHEN FINISHED.

Boot

Ball

Button

Battery

Answers on page 172

INVADER ALERT

1 Buzz is alerting Star Command about an invader. Use the code to work out who it is and write their name in the spaces below.

KEY: S D P L I H

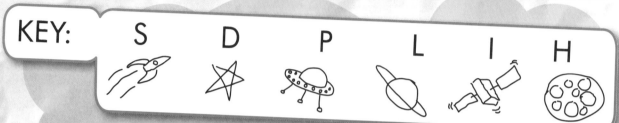

_ _ _ _ _ _ _ _ _ _ _ _

2 ## MISSION DEFENSE

Who has Buzz asked for help in order to defend the toys against the invader? Look at the close-ups below to find out.

Be on the lookout for strangers!

LIGHTYEAR

MISSION ACCOMPLISHED!

COLOR WHEN FINISHED.

Answers on page 172

ON A MISSION

Intrepid Buzz shows no fear when he is on a mission. Draw a line from each small picture to where it belongs in the big picture. Which picture doesn't belong?

MISSION ACCOMPLISHED!

COLOR WHEN FINISHED.

A

B

C

D

E

Answers on page 172

PLAYTIME FUN

The toys have been playing in the sandbox at Sunnyside Daycare. Have fun solving these puzzles.

A

① The toys are pretending they are on a beach.

Can you find and circle six differences in the bottom picture? There's one in each square.

B

WELCOME TO SUNNYSIDE, FOLKS!

2 Which two pictures of Woody and his ball are the same?

A
B
C
D

3 Jessie, Woody, and Buzz have been playing in the sandbox. Can you identify each character by their sand-shape?

A
B
C

WOODY

JESSIE

BUZZ

MISSION ACCOMPLISHED!

COLOR WHEN FINISHED.

Answers on page 172

BEFORE THE RACE

1 SAY CHEESE! RIPSLINGER LOVES POSING FOR THE PAPARAZZI. THERE ARE SEVEN DIFFERENCES BETWEEN THE TWO SHOTS OF THE RACER. FIND AND CIRCLE THEM!

2 A PASSION FOR BADGES!
EVERY RACER HAS TONS OF FANS, AND EVERY FAN WANTS TO SPORT HIS OR HER HERO'S BADGE. LOOK AT THE PILE IN THE BOX AND COUNT THE BADGES SOLD FOR EACH RACER. THEN WRITE THE NUMBERS IN THE BLANKS NEXT TO EACH NAME.

RIPSLINGER ...   **DUSTY** ...   **EL CHUPACABRA** ...

BULLDOG ...   **ISHANI** ...   **NED & ZED** ...

Answers on page 173

123

CHUG AND DOTTIE ARE WATCHING DUSTY ON TV. ADD SOME COLORS TO THIS SCENE.

RIPSLINGER ZOOMS THROUGH THE SKY.
ADD SOME COLORS TO THIS SCENE.
LET YOUR IMAGINATION SOAR!

PROPWASH GAMES

1 FILL HER UP, CHUG: STUDY THE SEQUENCE OF FUEL DROPS BELOW. IT APPEARS 4 TIMES IN THE GRID, FROM LEFT TO RIGHT—SEE THE EXAMPLE HERE. FIND AND CIRCLE THEM ALL.

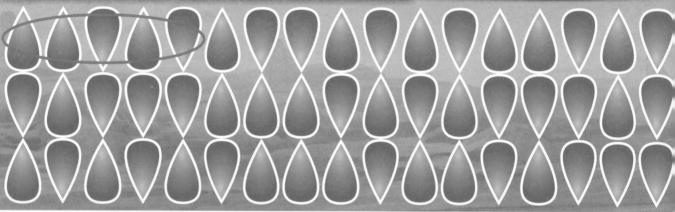

2 DREAMING OF THE RALLY: DUSTY'S **SPRAYING** A CORNFIELD AND DREAMING OF THE WATG. **COMPLETE** THIS SCENE BY **FILLING IN** THE **6 DETAILS** BELOW.

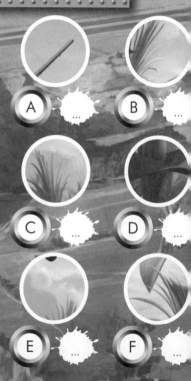

A ... B ...

C ... D ...

E ... F ...

Answers on page 173

126

START

FINISH

Answer on page 173

127

NEI-THER DID I!

THAT'S **IMPOSSIBLE!** I NEVER SAW THE MASTER LEAVE!

STRANGE!

HOLD THAT POSE FOR A SECOND ...

I'M SCARED...!

WE'D BETTER CHECK THE MASTER'S **CRYPT!**

YEAH! WE HAVEN'T TIDIED UP HIS **COFFIN** YET! IF HE FINDS THE BEDSHEETS IN A MESS, HE'LL GET MAD!

WELL, SINCE WE'RE NOT DISTURBING SOME VAMPIRE'S MEDITATION SESSION ... **COME ON!** LET'S FIND THE MAGIC BOOK!

THE LORD OF THE FANGS ... RECIPES: EASY BITES ... THE BETROTHED VAMPIRES ... SIGH!

POTIONS AND CAULDRONS! HEY, MAYBE THIS IS IT!

FFFF! DID YOU HEAR FETHRY SAY SOMETHING?

ACK! I'M SCARED OF DUST! IT HAS MITES!

Poof

FETHRY??

GASP! HE ... HE DISAPPEARED, TOO!

VERY FUNNY, COUSIN! DOES THIS REALLY SEEM LIKE THE TIME TO PLAY HIDE-AND-SEEK?

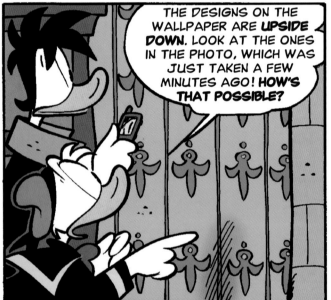

OUCH!

NICE LANDING, COUSIN!

PLOP

I PRESENT... **COUNT DRACUDUCK!**

SO YOU HAVE ALSO COME TO SHARE MY **SORRY FATE?** IT WON'T SOLVE ANYTHING, BUT AT LEAST I'LL HAVE SOMEONE TO PLAY **CARDS** WITH!

WHAT IS THAT MONSTER? **HOW** DID YOU END UP HERE?

I'LL TELL YOU...

TWO HUNDRED YEARS AGO, I WAS ABOUT **TO FIGHT** THAT CREATURE, THE **INFESTOR!** I HAD GONE TO THE LIBRARY TO FIND THE MAGIC BOOK THAT WOULD HELP ME CAST THE MYSTIC SNARE SPELL...

"...BUT THE MONSTER WAS **FASTER** THAN I WAS! IT HAD ALREADY INFILTRATED THE CASTLE BY CAMOUFLAGING ITSELF IN THE WALLS..."

POTIONS AND CAULDRONS

"...BUT IT ATTACKED ME **BEFORE** I COULD FINISH THE SPELL!"

"LUCKILY, I HAD ALREADY POSITIONED THE BOOK, SO THE MONSTER STAYED **STUCK** IN HIBERNATION IN THE LIBRARY..."

ZOT!

...BUT SINCE I'M STUCK HERE IN ITS STOMACH, I COULDN'T **FINISH** THE SPELL AND DESTROY THE CREATURE!

UM...WHAT DRACUDUCK HASN'T TOLD YOU YET IS THAT THE MAGIC BOOK WAS THE ONE THAT **I MOVED**...

...SO THE MONSTER **WOKE UP** FROM HIBERNATION!

GROWL

GASP! I'M AFRAID THERE'S ONLY ONE WAY TO SAVE MY FRIENDS... AND IT'S THE WAY THAT SCARES ME THE MOST...

...STAY HERE, NOT MOVING, LET MYSELF GET SWALLOWED BY THE WALL MONSTER...

CHOMP!

...AND HOPE THAT THE TRICK I WAS STUDYING...

...IN ORDER **TO GO THROUGH WALLS** WORKS!

GRAB MY HANDS! **QUICK!**

NOOOOOSH

VLUUP

VANISH! DISAPPEAR! RETURN TO THE SHADOWS FROM WHENCE YOU CAME!

WAIT A MINUTE! **BURNING** THE BOOKS WASN'T PART OF THE PLAN! AT LEAST, NOT PART OF **MY** PLAN!

IT'S OVER!

IT'S OVER FOR ME, TOO! **SIGH!**

WITHOUT THOSE BOOKS I CAN'T GET MY **COURAGE** BACK! MY CAREER AS A **MAGICIAN** IS OVER!

GET YOUR COURAGE BACK? TELL ME EVERYTHING!

FRIENDS, THIS ADVENTURE HAS MADE ME THINK! I'VE MADE AN IMPORTANT DECISION...

...THOUGH WHAT I SAY MIGHT SURPRISE YOU!

P.D.P. Television

WHAAAAT?! DUCKDINI THE MAGICIAN DOESN'T WANT TO DO THE SHOW ANYMORE?!

HE SAYS HE DOESN'T NEED TO DO DANGEROUS MAGIC **TO PROVE** HE HAS COURAGE!

AND HE'D RATHER **TEACH** THE SPECTATORS SIMPLE ILLUSIONS THAT THEY CAN USE TO ENTERTAIN THEIR FRIENDS!

QUACK! WHAT ABOUT MY CONTRACTS? **SNORT!** AND MY SPONSORS?

HEY! IT'S NOT OUR PROBLEM! TAKE IT UP WITH THE MAGICIAN!

HE COULD MAKE THEM **DISAPPEAR** BEFORE YOU HAVE TO PAY THE PENALTY!

END

TOY GAMES

AT BONNIE'S HOUSE THE TOYS RECEIVE UNEXPECTED NEWS...

THE SUNNYSIDE TOYS HAVE INVITED US TO PARTICIPATE IN THE FALL TOY GAMES NEXT SATURDAY?

BUT WE'LL NEVER BE ABLE TO WIN!

BUT WE HAVE A REAL SPACE RANGER! WE CAN WIN!

YES, WE CAN!

I'LL GIVE YOU LESSONS! I'LL TRAIN YOU! AND IN JUST ONE WEEK...

"...YOU'LL BE CHAMPIONS IN RUNNING..."

REX? WHAT ARE YOU DOING?

I WANT TO KNOW EVERYTHING ABOUT SPORTS, COACH LIGHTYEAR!

SPORTS RULES

"...RIDING OBSTACLE COURSES..."

NO! YOU MUST JUMP **OVER** THE OBSTACLE!

"...WEIGHT LIFTING..."

MAYBE IT'S BETTER TO START OFF EASY, WOODY...

"...AND SWIMMING!"

SIGH...

OKAY, WE STILL HAVE SIX DAYS!

THANKS TO BUZZ'S PERSEVERANCE...

WOW! I LOVE BADMINTON!

...AFTER A VERY LONG WEEK OF TRAINING...

GREAT JUMP, BULLSEYE!

...THE TOYS ARE READY FOR THE GAMES!

READY?

GOOOOO!

BUT...

I'M SORRY, BUZZ...THE FALL TOY GAMES GOT CANCELED BECAUSE OF THE SNOW!

OH NO...

WHY DID I LEARN EVERYTHING ABOUT BADMINTON THEN?

THE END

BONNIE'S SPA

THE END

Activity

Woody and the other toys have made Bonnie's bedroom into a Hawaiian getaway for Barbie and Ken. Can you find the Hawaiian words in the grid?

```
B A L O H A   A
V A U O O U   W
S L A J L   J
M X U I A S
D N E N E E
O K A I T S
```

Cross out the words when you find them. We've done the first one for you.

ALOHA!

~~ALOHA~~   LUAU

HULA   NENE

MISSION ACCOMPLISHED!

COLOR WHEN FINISHED.

Did you Know? Nene is the Hawaiian state bird!

Answers on page 173

DICE & JUMPS

1

ADD UP THE DICE

FIND THE PAIRS OF DICE OF THE SAME COLOR WHOSE SUM IS 7 (FOR EXAMPLE: 1+6, 2+5, AND 3+4) AND MARK THEM WITH AN X. THEN WRITE THE VALUE OF EACH REMAINING DICE BELOW AND ADD THEM UP.

6 + ... + ... + ... + ... = ...

TOTAL

JUMPING AROUND

Game

A GAME FOR TWO PLAYERS. PLACE PLAYING PIECES ON "START." TAKE TURNS ROLLING THE DIE, ADVANCE THE NUMBER OF SPACES SHOWN, THEN JUMP TO THE SPACE INDICATED. IF YOU JUMP TO AN ORANGE SPACE, MARK ONE POINT ON YOUR SCOREBOARD.

AND THE WINNER IS:
THE FIRST PLAYER TO EITHER REACH THE FINISH AREA OR COMPLETE HIS OR HER SCOREBOARD.

YOU WILL NEED A DIE + TWO PLAYING PIECES.

SCOREBOARD A

START

1
JUMP TO 20

2
JUMP TO 3

7
JUMP TO 1

6
JUMP TO 14

5
JUMP TO 12

4
JUMP TO 18

3
JUMP TO 21

8
JUMP TO 5

9
JUMP TO 7

10
JUMP TO 17

11
JUMP TO 13

12
JUMP TO 2

17
JUMP TO 11

16
JUMP TO 19

15
JUMP TO FINISH

14
JUMP TO 10

13
JUMP TO 4

18
JUMP TO 22

19
JUMP TO 15

20
JUMP TO 6

21
JUMP TO 9

22
JUMP TO 8

SCOREBOARD B

FINISH

24
JUMP TO 16

23
JUMP TO 24

CARSOLI'S GAMES

1

FIND THE CARS

FIND THE CHARACTERS BELOW IN THE CROWD.

LUIGI

GIUSEPPE MOTOROSI

FILLMORE

UNCLE TOPOLINO

2

COUNT THE TIRES

UNCLE TOPOLINO HAS LEFT HIS TIRES SCATTERED IN THE PIAZZA. HELP RETRIEVE THEM BY COUNTING U THE NUMBER OF EACH DIFFERENT COLOR, THEN WRITE THE TOTALS NEXT TO THE TIRES.

Answers on page 173

SMALL DETAILS

3 OF THE 4 DETAILS
BELOW COMPLETE THE
BLANKS IN THIS SCENE.
WHICH ONES?

A ...

B ...

C ...

D ...

TIRES

BLUE TIRE ...

GREEN TIRE ...

RED TIRE ...

Answers on page 173

ADD SOME COLORS TO THIS SCENE! TAKE INSPIRATION FROM THIS SHOT, OR LET YOUR IMAGINATION RUN WILD!

CARLA'S COLORS

I WEAR THE COLORS OF MY COUNTRY'S FLAG!

HERE ARE THE COLORS YOU'LL NEED:

 ORANGE
 YELLOW
 BLUE
 LIGHT GREEN
DARK GREEN
 BROWN
 DARK GRAY
 LIGHT GRAY

VARIOUS SECTIONS OF THE TRACK PUT MORE STRESS ON DIFFERENT PARTS OF A RACER. MATCH UP EACH PART ON THE RIGHT WITH ITS SILHOUETTE ON THE LEFT!

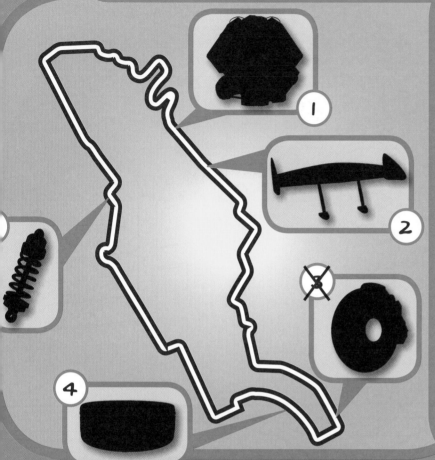

1

2

4

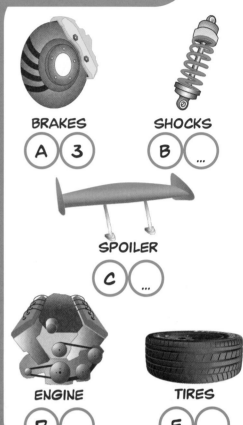

BRAKES   SHOCKS

A   3   B   ...

SPOILER

C   ...

ENGINE   TIRES

D   ...   E   ...

3 LIGHTNING SUDOKU

EACH ROW, COLUMN, AND MINI-GRID MUST CONTAIN ALL FOUR BACKGROUND COLORS. DON'T GUESS—USE LOGIC!

FIND THE RIGHT ORDER!

ADD SOME COLORS TO THIS SCENE! TAKE INSPIRATION FROM THIS SHOT, OR LET YOUR IMAGINATION STEER YOU!

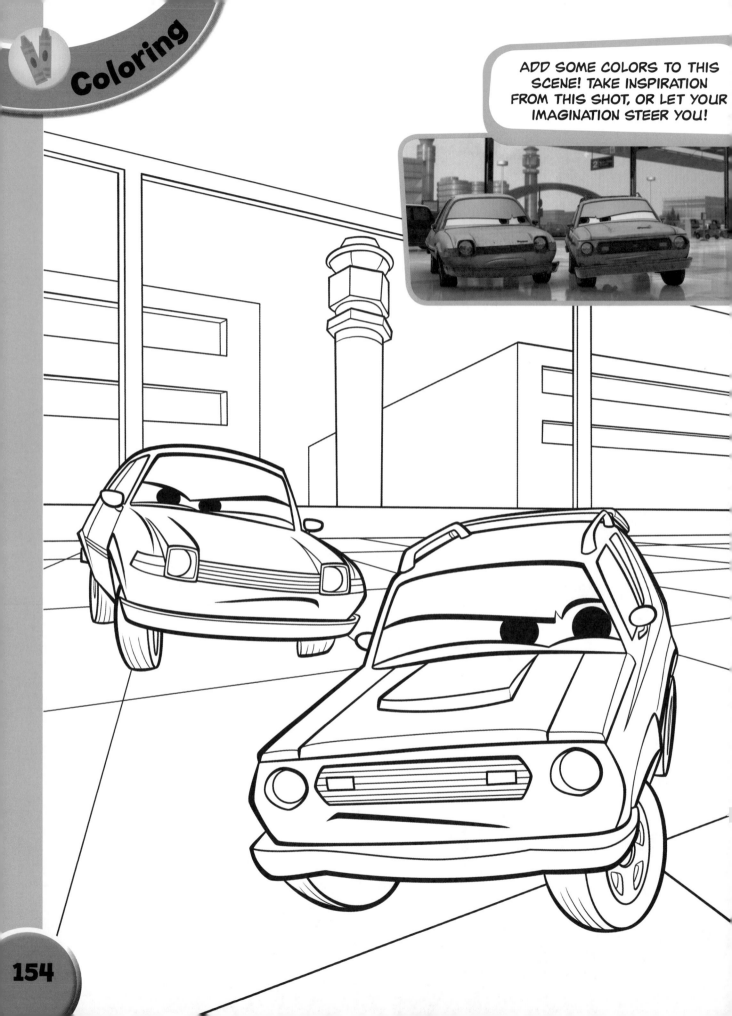

SHU'S COLORS

HERE ARE
THE COLORS
YOU'LL NEED:

 RED

 LIGHT RED

 DARK RED

 BLUE

 LIGHT BLUE

 DARK GRAY

GRAY

LIGHT GRAY

155

RACE TO THE BUST!

HIT THE TRAIL AND FIND OUT IF CANDACE CAN FINALLY CATCH PHINEAS AND FERB!

YOU'LL NEED

THREE PLAYERS
THREE TOKENS
A COIN TO FLIP

HOW TO PLAY

1. DECIDE WHO'LL BE PHINEAS AND FERB AND CANDACE. (FOR TWO PLAYERS, ONE PERSON CAN PLAY AS PHINEAS AND FERB AND THE OTHER AS CANDACE.) PLACE YOUR PLAYING PIECES ON YOUR START POSITION.

2. FLIP A COIN TO SEE WHO GOES FIRST. TO START, PLAYER ONE FLIPS THE COIN. FOR HEADS, MOVE FORWARD TWO SPACES. FOR TAILS, MOVE FORWARD ONE SPACE. FOLLOW THE INSTRUCTIONS ON EACH SPACE.

3. IF CANDACE LANDS ON PHINEAS'S OR FERB'S PIECE, THEY'RE BUSTED! BUT IF PHINEAS AND FERB MAKE IT AROUND THE BOARD AND BACK HOME WITHOUT CANDACE CATCHING THEM, THEY WIN—AND CANDACE MUST TRY TO BUST THEM AGAIN!

CANDACE START!

STOP TO CHAT WITH ISABELLA: LOSE A TURN.

SPEED BOOST FROM CHEETAH-FAST SHOES: MOVE AHEAD 1 SPACE.

STOP TO DANCE AT BEACH PARTY: MOVE BACK 1 SPACE.

WHERE'S PERRY?

LOSE A TURN.

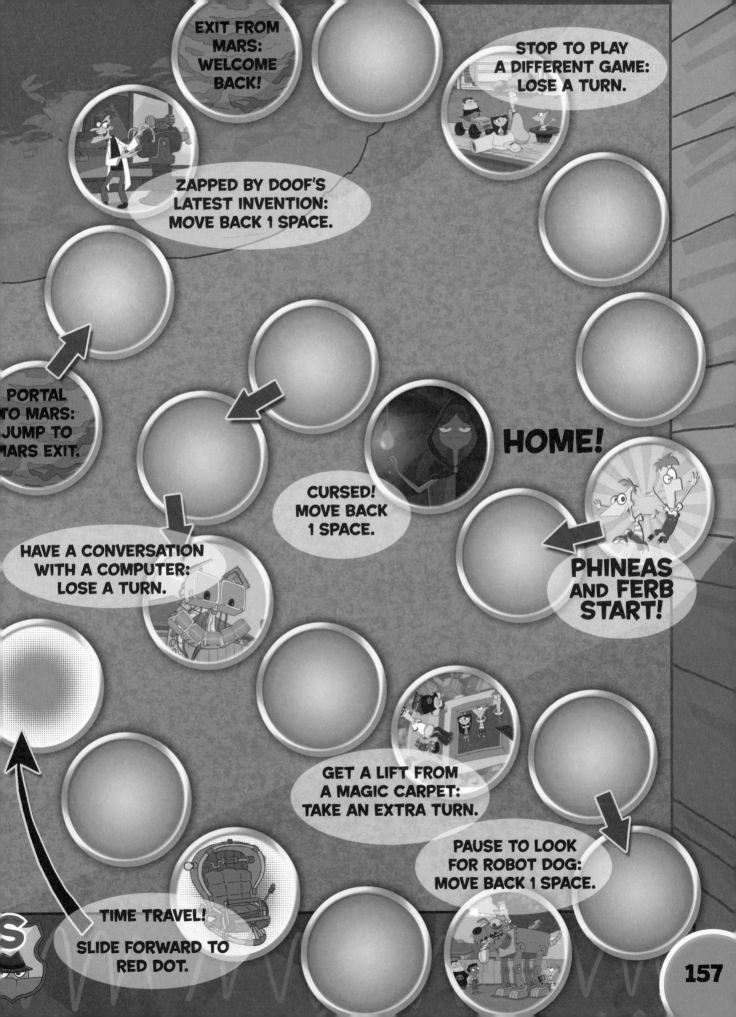

EXIT FROM MARS: WELCOME BACK!

STOP TO PLAY A DIFFERENT GAME: LOSE A TURN.

ZAPPED BY DOOF'S LATEST INVENTION: MOVE BACK 1 SPACE.

PORTAL TO MARS: JUMP TO MARS EXIT.

HOME!

CURSED! MOVE BACK 1 SPACE.

HAVE A CONVERSATION WITH A COMPUTER: LOSE A TURN.

PHINEAS AND FERB START!

GET A LIFT FROM A MAGIC CARPET: TAKE AN EXTRA TURN.

PAUSE TO LOOK FOR ROBOT DOG: MOVE BACK 1 SPACE.

TIME TRAVEL! SLIDE FORWARD TO RED DOT.

Inators
Gone Wild

DOOF'S INATORS HAVE GONE HAYWIRE (BIG SURPRISE!), WREAKING HAVOC ALL OVE
DANVILLE! SOLVE THESE PUZZLES TO RESTORE SOME ORDER TO THE TRI-STATE AREA

Copy Catastrophe

DOOF BUILT ANOTHER COPY-INATOR THAT MALFUNCTIONED AND STARTED MAKING COPIES
OF PEOPLE ALL OVER TOWN. CAN YOU SPOT THE ONE D'VILLER WHO WASN'T ZAPPED?

Answers on page 176

Combine and Conquer

GUESS WHAT HAPPENS WHEN DOOF FLIPS THE REVERSE SWITCH ON HIS COMBINE-INATOR! EVERYTHING FALLS APART, JUST LIKE THIS PICTURE. UNSCRAMBLE THE PIECES TO PUT IT BACK IN ORDER AND WRITE THE ORDER NUMBER OF THE PICTURES IN THE BOXES.

A.   B.   C.   D.   E.   F.   G.

Forget About It

DOOF'S AMNESIA-INATOR STRIKES AGAIN! AND THIS TIME, HE'S STRUCK HIMSELF WITH IT. UNSCRAMBLE THESE WORDS THAT ARE ALL IMPORTANT PARTS OF DOOF'S LIFE.

1. _ _ _ _
   NMRO

2. _ _ _ _ _ _ _
   SASNEAV

3. _ _ _ _ _ _
   ANIOTR

4. _ _ _ _ _ _
   THRWTA

5. _ _ _ _ _
   EORRG

6. _ _ _ _ _ _ _ _ _ _ _ _ _ _ _ _ _
   EPRYR HET YPSULPAT

7. _ _ _ _
   LEIV

8. _ _ _ - _ _ _ _ _ _ _ _ _
   RIT-TAETS RAAE

9. _ _ _ _ _ _ _ _ _ _ _ _ _
   RD. OLYDL REXLEW

10. _ _ _ _ _ _ _ _ _ _ _ _
    SEIRNSDULSTE

11. _ _ _ _ _ _ _
    TOECSLO

12. _ _ _ _ _ _
    GZOIMO

13. _ _ _ _ _ _ _ _ _ _ _
    HZTNODEISNPU

14. _ _ _ _ _
    GEONM

15. _ _ _ _ _ _ _ _
    OOLNBAYL

Answers on page 173

Fact or Fiction?

I'M HOME SICK TODAY, SO CARL HAS COME OVER TO READ ME A BEDTIME STORY. BU
THERE ARE TWO PROBLEMS HERE. FIRST, CARL ISN'T SUPPOSED TO KNOW WHERE I LIV
(THAT'S JUST CREEPY, CARL.) SECOND, CARL KEEPS CONFUSING THE DETAILS, AND NOW
I NEED TO FIGURE OUT THE TRUE STORY BY FINDING WHAT'S DIFFERENT BETWEEN THES
TWO PICTURES. SOME HELP YOU ARE, CARL!

Find All 13!

Answers on page 173

"Nice To Glow Ya"

TRAPPED LIKE A RAT IN A CAGE, PERRY THE PLATYPUS! OR–I GUESS–TECHNICALLY A PLATYPUS IN A CAGE, BUT THEN IT'S NOT REALLY A METAPHOR ANYMORE.

ANYHOO... BEHOLD! THE GLOWINATOR!

WHATEVER IT HITS WILL GLOW LIKE GANGBUSTERS...WHICH YOU MIGHT HAVE GUESSED FROM THE NAME... GLOWINATOR.

ZZZZAP!

SEE! IT WORKS!

AND NOW I'LL MAKE EVERY PERSON IN DANVILLE GLOW LIKE...LIKE SOMETHING THAT GLOWS!

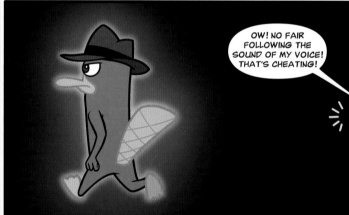

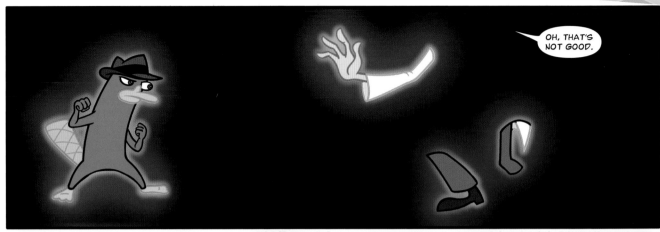

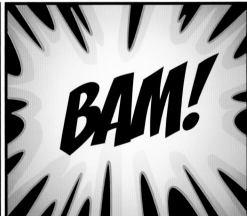

MULTICOLOR DISASTER

AHH RAMONE! WHERE ARE YOU GOING IN SUCH A HURRY?

OH NO! I'M LATE! LIGHTNING McQUEEN'S VICTORY PARTY IS ABOUT TO GET STARTED!

CONNECT THE DOTS TO DRAW OUR FRIEND LUIGI!

YES, I'M READY TO CLOSE UP AND HEAD OVER!

I WANT THE RIGHT LOOK FOR THIS PARTY. I REALLY WANT TO WOW EVERYONE!

THIS WON'T TAKE **LONG**, BUT I DON'T HAVE MUCH TIME!

NOT TO WORRY, MY FRIEND! AN ARTIST LIKE YOU WON'T HAVE ANY PROBLEMS...

RAMONE NEEDS YOUR HELP! LOOK AT THIS SPRAY GUN AND FIND WHERE IT'S HIDDEN IN THE SCENE!

OKAY... I NEED MY SPRAY GUN!

BONK

AND PAINT, TOO... OOPS!

SPLASH

Answer on page 173

167

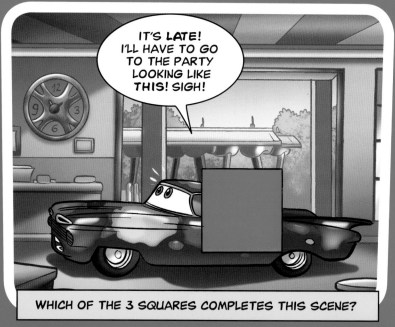

WHICH OF THE 3 SQUARES COMPLETES THIS SCENE?

Answer on page 173

AT THE PARTY...

LIGHTNING! HEY MAN, SORRY I'M LATE. I HAD A LITTLE...**ACCIDENT** WITH THE PAINT!

HEY BUDDY, YOUR NEW LOOK IS...

WHICH CHARACTER FROM THE SCENE DOES THE SILHOUETTE BELOW SHOW?

...AWESOME!

ARE YOU SERIOUS?

SUGAR, YOU ARE A WORK OF FINE ART!

YESSIR! JUST LIKE YOU'D DONE MEANT TO DO IT!

BUT I THOUGHT THIS WAS A FASHION DISASTER!

HA! HA! YOU MEAN A FASHIONABLE DISASTER!

The End

169

Answer on page 173

MIGUEL'S COLORS

MY NAME IS MIGUEL CAMINO!

HERE ARE THE COLORS YOU'LL NEED:

RED   ORANGE   LIGHT ORANGE   YELLOW   PEACH   GREEN   DARK GRAY   GRAY   LIGHT GRAY

Page 18

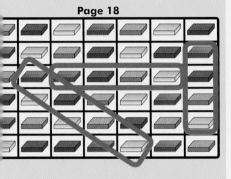

Page 19

Page 20

Page 21
Sushi Master: 1–D,E; 2–A,C,F; 3–B,G
kyo's Broken Lights: 1–D, 2–C, 3–A, 4–E, 5–B

Page 22
1–C, 3–A, 4–B
Dinosaur 2 does not have a shadow.
Rex is a Tyrannosaurus Rex.

Page 23

Pages 24–25
1–A, 2–C, 3–C, 4–B, 5–A, 6–B
The toy without a picture is Lotso.

Page 28
A–5, B–6, C–4, D–1, E–3, F–2

Page 29
A–1, B–5, C–4, D–2, E–3, F–6

Page 29

Page 32
A–1, B–5, C–3, D–4, E–2, F–6

Page 33
DUSTY—1ST
EL CHUPACABRA—2ND
RIPSLINGER—3RD

Page 52
RAOUL: 1+3+2+3+2+1+3 = 15
LIGHTNING: 3+2+1+2+1+3+2 = 14
FRANCESCO: 3+1+2+1+2+3+1 = 13

Page 53

1–D, 2–C, 3–A, 4–B

Page 54
IVAN

Page 55
Holo-Matching: D
Ivan's Tow-Maze: C

Page 56

Page 57

1–D, 2–B, 5–C, 6–A, 7–E
3 and 4 do not fit.

Pages 58–59

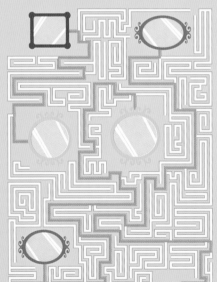

Page 61

1) YES
2) NO–Lotso says it.
3) YES
4) YES
5) NO–the Aliens say it.

Page 62

Page 63

Garden Friends: 1–G, 2–B, 3–D, 4–F, 5–C, 6–A
(E doesn't belong).
It's Showtime: D is the odd one out.

Page 65

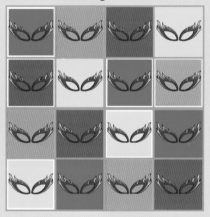

Page 86

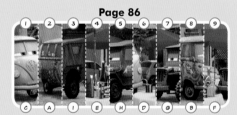

Page 87

Page 88

Pages 90–91

1: FIGHT AND FLIGHT
2: C is the odd one out.
3: A and C are exactly the same.
4: There is an ODD number of meteorites.

Pages 92–93

1: Etch A Sketch has finished the most drawings.
(Woody = 12, Etch A Sketch = 15)
2: D, A, B, C, E
3: PLAYTIME
4: LOTSO

Pages 94–95

Bravo–4, Dusty Crophopper–2,
Ripslinger–1, El Chupacabra–3

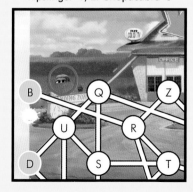

Page 97

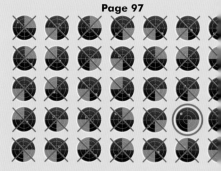

Pages 114–115

2: Footprint C is the largest.
3: There are four dinosaurs in total.

Page 117

Page 118

1: SID PHILLIPS
2: The green army men

Page 119

1–A, 2–C, 3–B, 4–E (D doesn't belong).

Page 120

Page 121

2: A and D are the same.
3: A–WOODIE, B–BUZZ, C–JESSIE

Page 122

Page 123

slinger = 4, Dusty = 7, El Chupacabra = 8,
Bulldog = 6, Ishani = 5, Ned & Zed = 2

Page 126

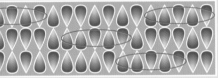

A–2, B–1, C–6, D–5, E–3, F–4

Page 127

Page 145

B	A	L	O	H	A
V	A	U	O	U	W
S	L	A	J	L	J
M	X	U	I	A	S
D	N	E	N	E	E
O	K	A	I	T	S

Page 146

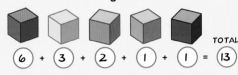

6 + 3 + 2 + 1 + 1 = 13 TOTAL

Pages 148–149

2: BLUE TIRE = 7,
GREEN TIRE = 5,
RED TIRE = 8
3: B–3, C–1, D–2 (A does not fit).

Pages 152–153
1: A–8, B–5, C–6, D–4, E–8
2: A–3, B–5, C–2, D–1, E–4

Pages 158–159
Copy Catastrophe: Buford
Combine and Conquer: G, A, D, B, F, E, C
Forget About It:
1. NORM
2. VANESSA
3. INATOR
4. THWART
5. ROGER
6. PERRY THE PLATYPUS
7. EVIL
8. TRI-STATE AREA
9. DR. LLOYD WEXLER
10. DRUSSELSTEIN
11. OCELOTS
12. GOOZIM
13. SPITZENHOUND
14. GNOME
15. BALLOONY

Page 160

Page 167

Page 168
Square 3

Page 169
Luigi